KT-196-693

DECEITFUL LOVER

'When you made the mistake of sharpening those long claws on a member of my family, you made everything about yourself my business.'

When the handsome stranger burst into Ria's flat and accused her of breaking his nephew's heart, she realised he had mistaken her for Poppy, her wayward cousin. Before Ria could explain, Dimitrios had forced her to accompany him to Greece to play the part of the happy fiancée for his family's benefit. Ria knew it was only a matter of time before Dimitrios discovered her true identity—and also that she had lost her heart to him...

DECEITFUL LOVER

Deceitful Lover

by
Helen Brooks

Magna Large Print Books
Long Preston, North Yorkshire,
England.

British Library Cataloguing in Publication Data.

Brooks, Helen
    Deceitful lover.

A catalogue record for this book is
available from the British Library

ISBN 0-7505-1128-1

First published in Great Britain by Mills & Boon Limited,
1992

Cover illustration © P. Gibson by arrangement with
Allied Artists

The moral right of the author has been asserted.

Published in Large Print 1997 by arrangement with Harlequin
Books SA.

Magna Large Print is an imprint of
Library Magna Books Ltd.
Printed and bound in Great Britain by
T.J. International Ltd., Cornwall, PL28 8RW.

For Clive, Cara, Faye and Benjamin

CHAPTER ONE

'Miss Quinton! I know you're in there, dammit! You have precisely sixty seconds to open this door before I break it down!'

Ria stumbled shakily into the small square hall of the flat, her ears ringing with the thunderous banging which had begun again immediately the harsh male voice had stopped. The front door was vibrating under the pressure of the savage blows being rained on it, and she could just imagine how her neighbours on either side were going to react to such a tremendous din at six o'clock in the morning. She'd already had a written list of complaints pushed through her letterbox awaiting her on her return after Poppy's occupation of her home while she'd been away. They were just going to love this!

'Right, young lady!' The furious voice rang out again just as Ria's hand slid the bolt on the door. 'Don't say you weren't warned!' At the same time as she wrenched open the heavy oak door a towering black shape cannoned into her, whipping the handle out of her fingers with incredible speed and sending her slim body spinning through the air to thud against the far wall with a loud thump.

'You stupid little idiot.' As she pushed back the thick mane of silky silver-blonde hair that had covered her face with the impact, she found herself being coldly scrutinised by one of the most ruthless faces she had ever seen. 'What possessed you to open the door like that? Haven't you got a grain of sense in that doll's head?'

The sheer injustice of the accusation provided the shot of adrenalin Ria needed to clear her whirling head and send the blood coursing angrily through her bruised limbs. 'How dare you?' She was relieved to hear that her voice was amazingly firm. 'You've been pounding away at my front door like some demented madman for the last few minutes and then you have the nerve to ask me why I opened it, to you...you...'

'If you are searching for an adequate description of me with your limited brain-power, please don't bother.' The malevolent voice was biting. 'You would be better employed asking me who I am, surely? Or maybe it is a common occurrence for you to open the door to strange men first thing in the morning?' Steel-blue eyes swept arrogantly over her body in scorching appraisal, and as his hard mouth tightened ominously his gaze became openly insulting.

'I don't care who you are,' Ria responded weakly, fear sending tiny shivers of panic down her spine. The thick fleecy robe she had pulled on so hastily had fallen open and the whisper-thin nightie she wore left nothing to the imagination. His cold narrowed eyes burned with contempt as he took in the full high breasts, slim waist and long shapely legs, seconds before she gathered the belt tightly round her body, jerking the ends violently, her hands shaking.

'You will care. Believe me, Miss Quinton, you will care.' It was a naked threat, the deep voice low and cruel.

Ria's frightened eyes darted to the open doorway behind him, but one glance at the stiff rugged face told her he had guessed her intention to run. His power was almost tangible; it oozed out of him, making her stomach muscles knot and her blood pulsate wildly. She had never been in the presence of such fierce masculinity before.

'What do you want?' Her soft grey eyes were huge in her pale face, her hands clenched nervously by her side.

'All in good time, my dear.' He pushed the door shut with the back of his foot, setting his tall lean body nonchalantly against the painted wood and crossing his arms slowly, his muscled frame perfectly relaxed. A heavy accent and the bronzed darkness of his skin told her he was not English but apart from that she had no clue as to who he was, or why he should be so fiercely angry with her.

His piercing eyes continued their leisurely wandering over her slight frame as she stood tense and still before him. 'Nice, very nice,' he murmured appreciatively, and as rich colour suffused her smooth honey-tinted skin in a red tide he smiled arrogantly.

'Eighteen, nineteen?' he asked calmly.

Ria frowned. 'I'm twenty-one, not that it's any of your business,' she said coldly, her face stiff.

'Oh, but it is my business, my cool little cat,' he corrected swiftly, his face

14

straightening. 'When you made the mistake of sharpening those long claws on a member of my family you made everything about yourself my business. The frequency with which you visit somewhat dubious nightclubs, your...regrettable lifestyle—'

'Now look here!' Ria cut in on the cold suggestive voice hotly, straightening her back as a pure white flame of anger swept through her. 'I don't know what you're talking about and I don't want to. I've never seen you before in my life and you think you can barge into my home, attack and insult me—'

The flow of words stopped as the stranger moved forward, calmly brushing past her with evident disdain and walking into the small compact lounge beyond.

'You had better come and sit down,' he suggested softly with just enough steel in his voice to make it a command. 'I am not in the habit of bandying words with women such as you. We have certain arrangements to discuss in the next hour and you will keep that beautiful mouth under control.' The big body was intimidatingly close.

'We have nothing to discuss,' Ria protested warily, edging carefully past him and subsiding thankfully into the

15

depths of an armchair. If only she hadn't opened the door; how could she have been so stupid? She was always so careful. It must be jet lag, she thought miserably to herself, watching him under her thick dark lashes as he swiftly checked each room of the tiny flat. She had been in America for six weeks coordinating an important photographic session, smoothing ruffled feathers when necessary, organising locations and ground-work and generally making sure everyone arrived at the right place at the right time. It had been exhausting but exhilarating—she loved her job as personal assistant to the boss of a small but exclusive modelling agency. She had arrived at Heathrow late the previous night, eventually dropping into bed in the early hours.

'It would appear we are alone.' The deep voice was expressionless, but Ria reared up like an enraged lioness.

'What did you expect?'

The soft laugh was mocking and totally without humour. 'We won't go into that, my dear Poppy. I can call you Poppy? I understand everyone else takes liberties with you.' He raised an authoritative hand as she went to reply, his expression

16

suddenly changing into splintered ice. 'Let us just get one thing absolutely clear at the start. I did not "barge" into your home, as you so charmingly put it, I have not "attacked" you, and if you feel the truth is insulting then perhaps it's time to take a long hard look at the selfish nasty little butterfly you are.'

Suddenly things were a little clearer. This madman thought she was Poppy. She groaned inwardly. What had her beautiful, unscrupulous and scatterbrained cousin been up to now? Her thoughts raced wildly. She had known it was a mistake to let her stay in the flat while she was away, but Poppy could be so persuasive with her velvet-brown eyes and persistent entreaties.

I've always been putty in her hands, thought Ria miserably, remembering Poppy's tenacity. There was someone special, the other girl had coaxed, and just a little time alone together would be heaven. Ria had had to admit the large house Poppy shared with five other girls was hardly conducive to romance. She always left there feeling shell-shocked.

'I can see light is dawning,' the foreign voice continued frostily, bringing her startled grey eyes up to his. 'Your face is really most expressive, my dear, not quite what I expected.' She glared at him silently, and he gave a dry chuckle.

'This time you pay for your mistake. You should be pleased. It will be yet another new experience for you to chalk up on your already undoubtedly long list.'

'Please listen, I must explain. You've got it all wrong—'

He interrupted her abruptly, his deep voice impatient. 'I'm not interested in anything you might have to say.' The cold eyes flicked over her disdainfully. 'You will be quiet and listen to me carefully. I have no intention of repeating myself.' He was obviously used to being obeyed and Ria felt too exhausted to retaliate further. In a confused daze she drew her small feet under her, huddling deep into the soft cushions like a small bewildered rabbit. Her fear must have communicated itself to the stranger, for his low voice was slightly less harsh when he spoke again, although the icy blue eyes never left her pale face for a moment.

'My name is Dimitrios Koutsoupis, I am Nikos's uncle,' he began, and at the lack of reaction on Ria's face his own hardened fractionally, anger etching the lines more firmly round his mouth and eyes. 'You do remember Nikos, I suppose?' he asked with heavy sarcasm, and as Ria stared at him silently he shook his black head in disgust.

'After you told him it was over between you he came home to Greece. He couldn't work, couldn't eat or sleep. Do you have any idea of what you did to him?' he questioned coldly. 'Was it really such fun to lead him on and then finish it in such a brutal fashion? Well, was it?' he suddenly snarled, her apparent impassiveness feeding his mounting rage and turning the narrowed eyes into steel-blue slits.

She looked at him silently, totally unable to think of a reply, and then shrugged her answer, the action taking on a coolness she hadn't intended.

'Priceless, absolutely priceless,' he ground out through clenched teeth, swinging around violently and striding across to the large window as though he couldn't bear to look at her a moment longer. He stood with his broad back to her, muscled legs astride and arms crossed, looking down into the already busy London street below, blazing anger apparent in every rigid line of his taut frame.

How long he stood there Ria didn't know. She kept quite motionless, completely at a loss as to how to placate this fiery Greek, her aching head trying to sort the few facts she had gleaned into some sort of order.

Obviously Poppy had indulged in one of her 'flings' as she called them. She had been left to pick up the pieces of those on more than one occasion, she thought grimly. Usually it was just lovesick phone calls from the rejected suitor pleading with her to ask Poppy to contact him, or being waylaid outside the flat or on her way to work by a heavy-eyed, dispirited young man asking what he had done wrong and begging for her help.

Invariably Poppy ended her romantic entanglements as if with the surgeon's knife, swiftly, cleanly and with no hesitation. Not again, Poppy, she breathed silently into the quiet room. You just can't resist it, can you? Over the last three years they had lived in London she had been a constant unwilling spectator, to the devastation her cousin's unique brand of cruelty caused. It sickened her even as she understood Poppy's consuming need for conquest and adoration.

Deep in thought, Ria started violently as Dimitrios turned from the window, his voice stiff and formal and the accent less pronounced now he had control over his feelings.

'I apologise for my behaviour,' he said unemotionally. 'I did not come here today to indulge my private thoughts or opinions; they are of little consequence.' He stood watching her, a lithe still figure impeccably dressed in a dark suit of excellent material, a red silk tie knotted casually at the collar of his spotless white shirt, a gold watch gleaming on his bronzed wrist. Everything about him suggested restrained strength and power.

'Why did you come?' asked Ria cautiously, feeling she had unwittingly let into her home a wild panther that might unleash its claws and spring for the death blow at any moment.

'I need your...co-operation.' The word was carefully chosen, she noted. 'Nikos's mother is not recovering as she should.' At her enquiringly raised eyebrows he stopped abruptly. 'You are obviously aware of the circumstances,' he stated frostily, and as she shook her blonde head in denial his amazed expression spoke for itself.

'I apologise again. In view of what Nikos has told me about your "intimate" relationship,' his lip curled on the word intimate, 'I naturally assumed you were familiar with his home circumstances. Normally in my country when rings are exchanged and promises given there are no secrets between a betrothed couple.'

Ria's dove-grey eyes widened apprehensively. There was much more to this than she had first imagined. She knew Poppy as well as she knew herself, and intimate relationships had never been on her cousin's agenda. As for rings being exchanged, the whole idea was ludicrous. What on earth have you done this time, you idiot? she asked her cousin silently, and why am I left holding the baby as usual? And what a baby! Six feet plus of determined steel.

'Nikos's mother, my sister Christina, has been seriously ill,' Dimitrios continued, running a large hand distractedly through his crisp hair as a flash of pain seared across the dark face. 'A bone disorder which is now under control. Unfortunately it has left her in severe pain and partially disabled. This will, in time, recede, but for the present it is vitally important that she retains the will to live and fight on regardless of the discomfort. The medication which is essential for her recovery also has an unfortunate side-effect causing acute depression. Warring factors!' He waved his hands latin-style, and Ria nodded understandingly.

'When Nikos announced he had fallen in love with an English girl his mother was naturally upset.' The harsh mouth tightened. 'A Greek girl would have been preferred, but we live in a modern age where young people choose their own destiny and often live to regret their mistakes.' He left her in no doubt that she was considered a grave mistake.

'However, within a short time it was apparent this...regrettable occurrence was proving of considerable benefit to my sister. Her one desire is to meet the girl Nikos has fallen so quickly and completely in love with, and see for herself that he will be settled and content with a suitable wife. It has given her a new interest at just the right time.'

Ria listened, her soft eyes puzzled. If Poppy had to all intents and purposes finished the relationship why had this big arrogant Greek travelled thousands of miles to talk to her?

'Christina is impatient to see you and I don't intend to disappoint her,' he finished in the same even tone, and it was a moment before she realised what he was insinuating.

As her head shot up and grey eyes clashed with blue he nodded lightly in confirmation. 'That's right,' he said quietly, cold amusement twisting his firm mouth in cynical satisfaction at her incredulous face. 'You will come to Greece with me and put on a magnificent show for my sister. You will convince her that you are a respectable and sweet young girl whose only aim in life is to make her son deliriously happy and provide him with a full quiver of fat bonny babies.'

'You're mad,' Ria breathed in horror, 'stark staring mad.' Strangely her reaction seemed to please him and he sat down opposite her, stretching out his long legs with a small sigh and leaning back with his hands behind his head.

'Of course it will depend on your acting ability as to when you return to England. I can understand it will be a difficult and demanding performance for someone like yourself,' the softly spoken words dripped venom, 'but try to look on it as a challenge to your already undoubted genius in that direction.'

Ria wouldn't have believed she could hate someone so strongly when she had been unaware of his existence an hour ago. The ache in her head had fixed itself into a dull thudding behind her eyes and a faint nausea was sweeping over her in waves. I must tell this maniac who I am, she thought weakly, rising to her feet in panic, but as she stood the room began to spin and turn and she sat down again abruptly, the colour draining from her pale face leaving it a sickly grey.

'For crying out loud.' The muttered words were full of irritation but the hand that pressed her back against the soft cushions was gentle. 'Overdoing the party life, no doubt.' She didn't have the strength to protest, merely shutting her eyes wearily and praying the threatening tears wouldn't betray her. One thing was sure, he had never seen a photograph of Poppy. Although the same age and height, they couldn't be more different. Poppy with her mass of flaming red curls and liquid brown eyes in sharp contrast to Ria's cucumber-cool English beauty. It would serve this bully right if he took the wrong girl back, she thought slowly; what a massive dent to his inflated ego.

As the faintness began to recede she opened her eyes cautiously to find his sombre face inches from her own. He immediately straightened from the crouching position at her side and stood looking down at her silently, a curious expression on his face and a small muscle jerking in his tanned cheek.

'Sit still.' The curt order had her clenching weak hands in frustration. She heard him moving about in the tiny immaculate kitchen and cupboard doors opening and shutting. 'Make yourself at home,' she called sarcastically, although the words came out less sharp than she would have liked.

A fresh steaming mug of strong tea was suddenly thrust under her nose. 'The British panacea for all ills, I understand,' Dimitrios said wryly as she automatically took the cup. 'I'm sorry that you appear to be in some genuine discomfort, for whatever reason—' he shrugged graphically '—but I have reserved two seats on the afternoon flight back to Greece, and you are coming with me if I have to carry you every single inch of the way.'

'I'm not coming anywhere with you,' Ria said flatly, sipping the scalding sweet tea gratefully as she tried to marshal her thoughts.

'It wasn't meant as an invitation.'

'An order, then? You're very good at those, aren't you? Well, if you think you can intimidate me you are picking on the wrong girl,' said Ria bravely. And the joke's on you, she added silently, glancing up at the inscrutable face defiantly.

He smiled slowly, the quality of the smile chilling her blood more than any words could have done. 'Take these.' He thrust two small white tablets into her hand.

She dropped them as though they had burnt her. 'What are they?' Her eyes were wide with fear. 'Where did you get them from? What are you trying to do to me?'

He sighed impatiently, obviously holding on to his temper by a thread. 'What do you think they are, you stupid girl? Aspirin from your kitchen cupboard. I may be involved in many activities but you can rest assured that drugs and slave-trading

27

are not on the list at the moment.' He bent and retrieved the tablets from the carpet, giving her a look of deep disgust as he vanished into the kitchen to reappear seconds later with the packet held between finger and thumb in his large hand. 'Here, help yourself, but just bear in mind you will be on that plane whatever it takes.' The deep timbre of that cool voice pulled at her nerves, sending a slow shiver down her spine. It was just as well she would never meet him again after today; his raw maleness affected her in the strangest way. It couldn't all be put down to jet lag.

The shrill tone of the telephone right by her side made her jump in fright, and she reached out a predatory hand before Dimitrios could lift the receiver, glancing at her watch as she did so. Seven o'clock? None of her friends would ring at this unearthly hour.

'Ria, oh, thank goodness, is that you? I've been counting the hours till you got back,' Poppy breathed down the phone, a sob breaking her voice. 'I'm in terrible trouble, you've got to help me.'

Vitally aware of the dark brooding presence across the room, his heavy-lidded eyes fixed on her troubled face, Ria forced herself to speak lightly. 'Hi, Sarah, only you could phone at this awful hour—another lift into work?' she improvised rapidly, turning in the chair so that her face was hidden from his implacable gaze. She felt this dark man with his foreign tongue could read her mind.

'Who's there, Ria?' The whisper held a note of sheer terror, sending her mind winging back in an instant through time. Two little girls playing in forbidden territory, balancing precariously on old lock-gates over the canal made slippy by a sudden summer storm. One child slipped and fell, and only the strength of the other prevented her from plunging into the murky water below and certain death. Poppy's voice had held the same note of fear that day but she had held on to her until help arrived, her arms groaning in the sockets. There was no way she was abandoning her now to this cold stranger.

'Sorry, Sarah, I can't really talk now. I'm not feeling too good.' Whatever Poppy had done to this man's nephew couldn't justify what he was asking of her. The whole idea was faintly pagan, some weird medieval sacrifice to appease the gods.

'What's happening?' It was the faintest of whispers.

'Yes, see you soon hopefully. Must go; Nikos's uncle is here all the way from Greece, would you believe?' The buzzing of an empty line in her ear told her Poppy did believe only too well.

'Bye, then, call me later.'

Dimitrios was sitting on the edge of a chair idly watching her as she turned round after replacing the receiver, his face shuttered. 'OK?' Ria wasn't sure to what he was referring but she nodded anyway. He had removed his tie and his shirt was open several buttons from the throat revealing dark curling body hair. A thin trickle of something akin to excitement snaked up her spine and she gulped noisily.

'That was Sarah,' she proffered unnecessarily and he nodded slightly, contemplating her with cold eyes that betrayed nothing.

'You have exactly five hours before we need to leave for the airport,' he said shortly. 'I suggest you use them wisely. If you need to consult a doctor for medication I shall be happy to arrange it. Otherwise put your affairs in order and assume you may be away some time.'

'This is absolutely ridiculous,' she began in alarm. 'I have my work and the flat; you can't expect—'

'Oh, but I do expect.' Dimitrios looked hard at her, his square jaw tightening. 'For once in your life you are going to do exactly as you are told.'

'Just who do you think you are, anyway?' she countered helplessly.

His mouth moved in a smile of cold satisfaction. 'I have told you who I am, and I know what you are.' As she caught her breath in frustration he continued, 'A model, I understand? Nikos tells me you are quite in demand.' He managed to make his words sound infinitely distasteful. 'You are quite used to the possibility of leaving the country at short notice for your work, which incidentally is of no importance to me. My sister however is of supreme importance and I intend to see she has complete peace of mind about you. You will play the part of loving fiancée to my nephew for as long as it takes.'

It was as though she were beating her hands against solid rock. 'You've got this all wrong.'

He lifted one dark brow. 'Yes?' His

31

gleaming eyes narrowed scornfully as she hesitated. 'Does it tempt the jaded palate if I explain it is an all-expenses-paid trip including reimbursement for your work? What figure fits the bill, I wonder?' He named a sum of money that made Ria's eyes widen and dark colour flood her pale face.

'You're trying to buy me.' There was a note of horrified wonder in her voice. 'What sort of people are you used to being with?'

His eyes snapped wide open as his face froze into granite. 'It is dangerous to push me too far, Miss Quinton. I am a good friend but a bad enemy. You will never count me among the former, but just pray I don't make it my business to become the latter.' He moved in front of her as he spoke, his virility almost tangible, a live magnetism that fascinated her even as it repelled her.

She wanted to move, to back away, but was frozen like a small mouse transfixed before its predator. 'Keep away from me, you just keep away from me.'

'I don't think you are in any position to give orders.' His face was faintly cruel. 'Do you?'

She stared at him fiercely, her grey eyes stormy. 'What will you do if I disobey you? Hit me? Is that the sort of man you are, brute strength and—?'

'How dare you presume to judge me?' His voice was a snarl and his eyes were suddenly chips of ice. 'Someone like you...' In one lithe movement he pulled her roughly against his hard body, turning her deftly so that she was pressed against the wall, imprisoned by his superior strength.

'There are many different ways to teach a little alleycat like you some manners.' He lowered his head as he spoke, his warm breath fanning her white face. She struggled madly to break his iron grip as his mouth sought hers, and he chuckled deep in his throat as she twisted her head from side to side. 'You like your men subjected and adoring, no doubt. Poor Nikos never stood a chance, did he?'

As his kiss burnt along her throat she knew sheer animal panic, kicking out wildly with her legs and wrenching at the steel arms that held her body so tightly. He made a sound of annoyance against her hot cheek, bending her backwards, his pressure irresistible, until she had to cling on to him for support as her back muscles screamed.

His mouth moved sensuously over hers, parting her lips with expert control and plundering the warm interior of her mouth slowly and firmly. Her heart began to pound as the kiss went on and on, a flood of emotion sweeping over her that frightened her more than his embrace. She had never realised that a kiss could be so intimate; the few friendly goodnight kisses she had shared with the odd boyfriend in the past hadn't prepared her for anything like this, or warned her that her senses could run wild.

She beat frantically with her small fists against his muscled back as his mouth moved back to her throbbing throat, a choking sob breaking her voice. 'Don't, please don't.'

He slowly raised his bent head, his expression quizzical. 'You sound as if you mean that.'

'I do, I do!' She was almost incoherent with fear, aware of the compressed power in every steel line of his big frame.

He moved her to arm's length, looking down consideringly into her terrified eyes. 'I thought you were a big girl,' he said gently, something unreadable in his dark face. 'You'll have me believing you're not used to this if you're not careful.'

'You were hurting me,' she whispered shakily, pushing back a tendril of silver hair from her face with hands that shook.

'I was?' he said sceptically, his eyes sweeping over her flushed face, and then in a lighter tone, 'I must be losing my touch. I don't normally get this reaction when I kiss a woman.'

Ria was convinced. Those few minutes in his arms had brought alive to her for the first time man's age-old dominance over woman. Her skin was still crawling with a strange thrill and as she broke away from his hold he let his arms fall by his side, something burning deep in his hooded eyes.

'Well?' The word was sharp and heavy with meaning; he had returned to the attack immediately. 'Do I pack your belongings for you, or are you going to pull yourself together and be sensible?'

She shrugged, flushing. For the first time she found herself considering his ridiculous order seriously. What could he do to her after all? She wasn't Poppy, she would have the last word, but in the meantime it would give her cousin a valuable breathing-space. Poppy would be no match for this man.

'I do have some holiday outstanding,' she murmured quietly. It was true, she had only taken one week of last year's entitlement, and there had never seemed time to fit the residue in. She could leave a message for Poppy with her modelling agency explaining what she had done, her passport was up to date thanks to the American trip and she had no immediate commitments. It would only be a short-term solution but it was better than throwing her cousin to the wolves, or to one wolf in particular.

She looked up slowly and nodded confirmation as she met his penetrating gaze. 'I'll come,' she said woodenly, 'but don't say I didn't try to warn you you're making a terrible mistake.'

An almost savage look of triumph flashed across the cold features, swiftly masked. What have I done? she asked herself weakly. What have I done?

CHAPTER TWO

The first-class accommodation on the plane was wonderfully luxurious and in any other circumstances Ria would have enjoyed every moment, but the implications of her actions were crowding in on her, making her mouth dry and her palms wet.

If I thought Dimitrios was crazy, what does this make me? she asked herself miserably, risking a quick glance at the silent figure at her side. As soon as they had been airborne he had stretched out his big frame comfortably in the soft padded seat, eyes closed and body relaxed. With a tingling shock she saw that the piercing blue eyes were fixed thoughtfully on her face.

'Isn't it uncomfortable?'

'What?' She thought she had misheard the quiet words.

'The "do not disturb" sign hanging round your neck.'

She stared at him, bewilderment making her soft grey eyes huge. 'I don't know what you mean,' she said carefully, her voice stiff.

'Now I don't know if I believe that.' The discerning cold eyes probed her pale face. 'I was expecting a flamboyant virago who would try to use either charm or feminine cunning to get her own way, and I find a cool aloof ice-maiden instead.' He shook his dark head consideringly. 'It's a clever tactic. Perhaps my prediction was a little obvious.'

Ria held his gaze nervously. His insight into Poppy's character had been totally accurate. It was exactly how she would have reacted. She must be more careful; this vibrant powerful man was frighteningly perceptive.

She shrugged her eyes away from the penetrating hold.

'I'm not responsible for your suppositions,' she muttered. 'I suppose you're one of those male chauvinists who think all cats are grey in the dark.'

'Not quite.' The deep voice held a thread of laughter. 'I try to keep an open mind, but it isn't easy.'

An attractive blonde stewardess placed the long iced drink she had ordered in front of her, cutting off further conversation. Ria smiled her thanks but the carefully made-up eyes were on the dark man at her side, an expression of almost hungry desire on the pretty face.

'Anything I can get you, sir?'

The girl was positively drooling, Ria thought irritably, but it seemed to make no impact on Dimitrios. 'No, thank you.' He smiled dismissively, his face distant and uninterested. He settled back in his seat again, shutting his eyes. In repose his features lost the austere coldness they assumed normally and she noticed white lines of fatigue around his mouth and eyes. She wondered idly how old he was, thirty—thirty-five perhaps, but the chiselled face and hard lean body gave nothing away.

'I can give you a signed photograph if you'd like.' She started as the smooth sardonic voice drawled quietly by her side, his eyes still tightly shut. 'But I can understand that you like to look at the real thing.'

'Oh, you're just a...a...'

He chuckled maliciously as she floundered for words. 'I think I get the drift without further splutterings. You still look a little pale; why don't you shut your eyes for a while?'

'I'll shut them when I'm ready,' she retorted childishly, and the low deep chuckle sounded again, doing strange things to her insides.

She lay back in her seat, eyes stubbornly wide open. She would have liked to have taken his advice; her head ached and she felt as though she was suffering from the worst attack of flu she had ever experienced. Jet lag. It didn't help to know the cause. If I never see the inside of another plane in my life it will be too soon, she thought dismally. Events had moved with incredible swiftness since her capitulation to his demands that morning, and she was now too exhausted to sleep.

'Do you have any family?' His voice was mildly conversational and for a moment she almost shook her head, lulled into a false sense of security. Her own parents and baby brother had been killed in a horrific car crash when she was seven, and Poppy's father had taken his brother's only surviving child into his home as company for his difficult daughter, his wife having died two years previously.

'My father lives in Essex and I have a

40

cousin in London.' How she hated lying; her voice shook slightly and she made an effort to pull herself together. This would never do.

'Ah, yes, Nikos mentioned your father.' His voice was condemning. 'I understand you don't get on with him; you find him too authoritative perhaps?' There was no doubt where his sympathy lay.

'I suppose so.' She looked at him warily.

'Poor man.' The words were dry.

'You've never met him, so reserve your opinion,' she said sharply, a picture of Uncle John's cold aloof face flashing into her mind. He had always tolerated her with cool detachment, but to Poppy he had displayed an almost cruel coldness which had resulted in his spirited daughter's outrageous bids for affection as long as she could remember.

'I've met you and that's enough,' Dimitrios said softly, the steel back in his voice. 'I'm sure you can always find an excuse for your unprincipled behaviour, and when all else fails it's convenient to land it all back at Daddy's door, isn't it?'

'It isn't like that,' she replied fiercely, although a voice inside her acknowledged that there was a grain of truth in what he said.

'Really?' His voice was faintly bored. 'Convince me.'

She looked into the cynical, mocking face despairingly and slumped back in her seat feeling totally drained. 'Oh, what's the use?' she muttered. 'You wouldn't believe a word I said.'

'How perceptive.'

She glared at him, rebellious hate turning her eyes into shining slate.

'I've known countless women like you, my dear,' he said contemptuously. 'Spoiled from an early age with too much of everything, you are far from unique.'

Her cheeks burned angrily but she warned herself to say nothing. It would be too easy to give herself away on such an emotive subject. She remembered how thrilled Poppy had been to see her when she first went to stay. The two little girls, totally different in temperament, had had an immediate rapport, drawing from each other the affection they craved. Theirs had been an isolated, lonely childhood in the old rambling country house but they had had each other and that had sufficed, running wild most of the time and attending the tiny village school only when necessary.

The solid country folk had grown used to seeing two small girls, one waif-fair with long silky locks flying behind her and the other cheekily gamine with gleaming copper curls and laughing brown eyes, roaming the sweetly scented lanes and meadows at all hours of the day or night.

She smiled faintly in remembrance and the man watching her caught his breath, his expression darkening.

'Who's brought that smile to your lips?' he asked harshly. 'Another poor fool you played your games on?'

She stared at him, caught by the bitterness in his voice, unaware of the tender softness the childhood memories had brought to her face.

'Oh what's the use?' he ground out savagely. 'You sicken me with your cheating little mind. What am I wasting my breath for?' The unprovoked attack left her speechless with its ferocity and she shrank back in her seat, white and shaken. He gave her a look of utter contempt and shut his eyes again, his body gradually relaxing in the seat, until his steady breathing told her he was asleep.

She sat hardly daring to move, every muscle in her body throbbing and a dull ache in the back of her head. She had never felt so ill or alone in all her life. Suddenly a rush of hot tears forced their way through her tightly closed eyelids, stinging her eyes and blocking her nose. What a mess, what an awful mess, she thought disconsolately, giving a forlorn little sniff and burying her head in the seat.

A large crisp white handkerchief appeared under her nose and Dimitrios's hand gently turned her quivering chin round to face him while he mopped her face quietly. 'Assimenios, assimenios' he muttered softly under his breath. 'Why the tears?'

Ria gulped deep in her throat, quite unable to stem the flow, and after a moment he drew her closely against him so that she was lying across the seat, cradled against his broad chest.

In spite of her humiliation a soft warmth spread through her aching limbs, comforting and dulling her mind. 'Relax, little one, shut those wickedly beautiful eyes.' His murmur was almost inaudible and again held that thread of mocking laughter but this time she didn't care. It was so intoxicating to feel the rhythmic steady beat of his heart, the sensual combination of masculine strength and tenderness.

'Poor baby, all worn out...' The soft voice was incredibly soothing, mingling with the spicy tang of expensive aftershave and a slight aroma of cigar smoke on his jacket. She found the warm glow sharpening to a twisting throb in her lower stomach and had the crazy desire to open his shirt and lay her soft cheek against the dark hair covering his chest. The impulse became overwhelming, a hot shudder shaking her body and causing her to rear up in self-recrimination and move quickly back into her own seat, flushed and trembling. If he noticed her agitation he made no comment. After one swift searching glance he lay back, eyes shut, perfectly relaxed and controlled.

'Quite a mixture, aren't you?' The deep voice was dry and cool. 'I was wondering how long you would be able to keep the ice-maiden act going.'

He was playing with her! He was quite aware of the effect he had on her and found it amusing.

'I hate you,' she whispered tightly, her

hands clenching by her side.

'Why? Because I'm up to all your little wiles?' He didn't open his eyes as he spoke and his profile could have been cut in granite. 'Believe me, my faithless little siren, you just aren't in the big girls' league. Try your tricks on me at your own peril.'

She raised her head proudly. There was no retort she could make without making him suspicious but it hurt to be so misjudged. The very fact that she and Poppy were so unalike in character had kept them close over the years; living on the fringe of her cousin's whirlwind was all the excitement her quiet, reticent nature needed.

'How much leave did your boss give you?' His voice was quietly conversational again. The man was as changeable as a chameleon.

'As much as I need,' she answered curtly, unable to match her tone with his.

'Really? You are obviously on good terms with him.'

'What does that mean?' she asked warily, not fooled by the soft voice. She had seen his eyes snap open.

'What should it mean? Guilty conscience?' He eyed her keenly, taking in the slow flush staining her cheeks.

'He's a friend, that's all,' she replied coldly, a shutter coming down over her eyes. 'Merely a friend.' She wasn't going to discuss Julian with this unfeeling monster. Julian Brand had taken a massive gamble when he had given her the chance to be his right-hand 'man' in his small thriving business. There had been several other applicants far more qualified and experienced, but he had seen the fervour and hope in her eyes and also the misery that working in front of the camera was causing. She had been employed with Poppy by one of his competitors at the time, dying a little every time the catwalk forced her to quell the innate shyness that was an integral part of her.

'Three months, darling,' Julian had smiled, his effeminate appearance hiding a brilliant photographer and astute businessman. 'Three months to prove yourself and then I throw you back to the wolves if you're no good.' He rarely made mistakes and he hadn't made one with her. When the three months were up he had doubled her salary, blessing the sixth sense that had guided his choice. She had worked sixteen-hour days for the first six months, loving every minute and rapidly becoming vital to the small company's growth. What she had lacked in experience she had made up for in effort. Now, two years later, Brand's Agency had a reputation for excellent value and first-class efficiency.

'Would this be one of the "friends" you dance the night away with fairly frequently?' the deep voice persevered, intruding into her thoughts.

'Maybe,' she answered non-committally, an unconscious gleam in her eye at the vision of Julian dancing the night away with any female. She occasionally shared a meal with her boss and his flatmate Kelvin, but the agency took all her spare energy often keeping her working into the early hours. She preferred it that way. Romantic entanglements were not for her; she had never met a man who had remotely stirred her blood and had begun to believe Poppy was right, that she was frigid. That was one myth she could now dispel.

'How can a nice little girl like you afford a place of her own in London?' He had clearly changed his line of attack. 'The rent must be exorbitant.'

'I don't pay any rent.' Ria spoke quickly without thinking. 'I own the flat.'

He sat up abruptly, all pretence at resting vanishing. 'Well, well, well.' The suggestion was unmistakable. 'And there was me wondering if I'd made things awkward for you at work.' He gave her a glance that froze the blood in her veins, a red glow deep in the narrowed eyes. 'Did Nikos know about your...arrangement?'

'There is no arrangement,' she said flatly, lowering her eyes to her lap. 'If you must know, the money I used was left to me, although I don't know why I'm bothering to explain myself to you.'

'Explain yourself!' The words were a low hiss, making her jump. 'Don't insult my intelligence, Miss Quinton. That explanation might have sufficed to convince my nephew but I am no naïve youth to be taken in by your lies. Nikos is my responsibility since his father died and I won't have him mixed up with a...a...'

'With a what?' Ria taunted furiously, her face as angry as his. She was sure he would have hit her if they hadn't been on a plane several thousand feet up in the air surrounded by people.

'I'm sure you know the name for that

49

profession as well as I do.' The words crackled in the air.

Ria looked at his face black with rage. How much did he know about Poppy's history? How could she explain that her uncle had bought her the flat with the residue from her father's estate that had been held in trust for her until she was eighteen? She stared dumbly at him, her mind racing, until he turned away in disgust, his full moulded lips curling back from his teeth.

'Incredible, quite incredible,' he muttered bitterly, levering his big frame out of the seat. 'All that wantonness concealed behind such a pure façade. I made a mistake; you are into the big girls' league after all.' He went to move down the aisle and then leant back over her seat, his face close to hers. 'You know, you had me feeling like some sort of lecher back there in England. Next time there will be no brake applied; you will get exactly what you ask for, so just be careful. I'm not some young boy to be led along by the nose.' It seemed as if the devil himself was looking out of those merciless eyes and Ria shrank back in her seat, her heart leaping into her throat.

The Greek airport was small, dirty and exceedingly hot. The humid air that enveloped her as soon as the doors of the plane opened reeked of oil and fumes, and Ria stumbled down the steep steps half asleep and feeling dazed and sick. She was still trembling from the confrontation with Dimitrios, although an icy silence had prevailed since he had slid back into his seat smelling strongly of whisky.

'Get in.' The sleek white Ferrari had been parked just outside the air terminal and apprehensively she slid inside. The black upholstery smelt of real leather and as the engine purred into life she risked a little sidelong glance at his rigid face.

'How far have we got to go?'

'As far as it takes.' He was obviously not going to meet her halfway.

The sky swiftly became a black velvet blanket patterned with a myriad tiny twinkling stars, peaceful and serene, but the atmosphere inside the car was electric. A few miles from the airport Dimitrios turned the low powerful car into the hills, and they had been steadily climbing a narrow bumpy road for some time before he swung into a small car park at the side of the track.

Ria stared at him warily as he leant back with a sigh in the seat, his large hands resting on the top of the leather-bound wheel.

'Don't keep looking at me as though I am going to eat you alive.' The words were low and thick, and a muscle near his mouth jerked ominously. 'I thought you would like some refreshment before we continue our journey.'

Opening the car door, he helped her out, his light touch on her arm sending small warning ripples to her senses. The small courtyard was empty except for a tiny ornate dovecote and a few scattered wooden benches and tables, and the air was beautifully cool. Dimitrios disappeared through the arched doorway to return almost immediately with two long fruit-filled drinks in which ice clinked tantalisingly.

'How do you feel?' The vivid blue eyes raked her pale face swiftly.

'I don't know,' she returned stupidly, longing to place her aching head on the rough wooden table and sleep in the scented air.

He sat down carefully, avoiding touching her as he stretched his long legs under the intricately carved table. She looked at him nervously, his finely chiselled face thrown into stark relief by the shadows.

'You are frightened of me—why?' he asked slowly as he caught and held her glance. 'Is it because of our conversation on the plane?' The strong firm mouth grimaced slightly. 'On reflection I was maybe a little severe. I don't know where you got the money from to buy your own place and I don't want to know,' he added shortly, holding up his hand as Ria went to speak. 'However, I don't think you are a woman of low repute so we'll let the matter end.'

'Why don't you think I'm...what you said?' Ria asked curiously, her eyes steady.

'Let's just say I've had enough liaisons in my life to know when I'm dealing with an accomplished courtesan,' Dimitrios said drily, 'and that you certainly are not.' Ria flushed hotly, remembering her undisguised panic at his lovemaking.

'They don't normally do that either,' he said softly, stroking a mocking finger over her hot cheek. The light touch caused a hundred muscles to constrict in her traitorous body and she jerked away sharply, causing him to chuckle deep in his throat.

'Oreos, oreos,' he whispered slowly, the small courtyard suddenly becoming uncomfortably intimate as his eyes roved over each feature of her face, his gaze curiously rueful.

'What does oreos mean?' Ria asked brightly, gulping at her drink nervously, striving to break the mood that had sprung up between them.

'Oreos? Come come, my sweet, I'm sure you've heard that word before,' Dimitrios said quietly, the atmosphere imperceptibly changing. 'I can't believe Nikos didn't tell you how beautiful you are, how those soft grey eyes entice and then retreat until they could drive a man mad, how your lips—'

'Stop it,' she pleaded, her voice shaking. 'Please, Dimitrios.'

'That's the first time you have spoken my name,' he said gently, making the words into a soft caress. 'It wasn't too bad, was it?' His dark shape seemed at one with the shadowed courtyard, his white teeth gleaming in the blackness.

Ria stood up quickly, knocking the last of her drink over in her haste. The tall glass smashed on to the small cobbles, shattering into a thousand tiny splinters, the harsh sound jarring the cool air with raucous harshness.

'Oh, I'm sorry,' she gasped, backing away against the whitewashed taverna wall, the mellow stones still warm from the fierce heat of the day.

Dimitrios calmly unfurled his legs from under the small table, his mocking blue eyes never leaving her flushed face for a moment. 'Why the hurry, my little dove?' he said blandly, lifting her chin up firmly with one hand so that she was forced to look into his dark face, curling his other arm possessively round the small of her back. 'I thought you liked to hear how you please men's senses, how easily you can capture their poor hearts.'

As he had been talking his arm was drawing her inexorably closer into his hard body like a band of steel until her soft curves were moulded into his maleness, so close that she could detect the intoxicating lemony smell of his warm skin. 'Or is it just this particular man you have an aversion to?'

She was effectively pinned between the taverna wall and his tall hard frame, any movement she made grinding the contours of her body against his.

'You are a mass of contradictions. Is this all part of the game? This shy naïveté a clever act to keep your men on their toes? It's a fine dividing line you're treading, but I have to admit it's appealing. Yes, very appealing,' he added, his finger outlining the shape of her quivering lips.

'Please let me go,' she whispered brokenly, conscious of a heat enveloping her thighs and stomach, a slow sweet throbbing she had never experienced before. He gazed down at her, enigmatically foreign, and as she began to struggle in his inflexible hold she felt his body responding to her movements and heard his sharp intake of breath between clenched teeth.

He slowly lowered his black head over her, brushing cool lips coaxingly over her exposed throat and ears. A light shiver of pure excitement washed over her body, setting every pulse tingling with life, and she tried in vain to hold on to her emotions, desperately quelling this need that was threatening to drown her. 'Don't,' she whispered weakly as a primitive reaction had her arching instinctively against his body, causing him to growl deep in his throat.

His experienced hands skilfully stroked her back, drawing her gently against him again and again in soft rhythm, slowly undermining any resistance while his hard lips parted hers in a deep scorching kiss that seemed to draw her soul out of her body in a low moan. The sweet ache became a dull pain, destroying her ability to think or reason, and she trembled helplessly in his arms, every nerve-end vitally alive.

It was a moment before she realised she was free again, that his light hold on her quivering body was merely supportive. He raised his head consideringly, narrowed eyes mocking. 'Mmm, definitely most appealing,' he said softly as he took a step backwards, dropping his arms by his side, 'but maybe a little dangerous too.' He stared at her intently, his expression unreadable. 'Poor Nikos.'

She stared at him dumbly, too shaken to respond, an untouched section of her brain noting with resentment how perfectly in control he seemed while she could hardly stand.

'Clever little minx.' It was as though he

were talking to himself, his eyes on her but not seeing her. 'The ice-maiden melts and makes you think it's just for you—quite an act to beat, I have to admit.'

He had no idea his murmured words were hitting her like blows. He thought it was all an experiment, that she reacted to any man's lovemaking like this. As the thoughts penetrated her dazed mind she looked deep into his eyes and saw an icy coldness there, cynical contempt in every line of his relaxed body. He thought he had succeeded, got her all taped in that smooth unfeeling brain.

She moved quite silently, taking him completely by surprise. As her hand made contact with his face his head was jerked back violently; she had put all her weight behind the blow. For a second time seemed to stand still in the dark perfumed air, the sound of the mini-explosion vibrating in the blackness. His incredulous expression would have been quite comical in any other circumstances, but as her red handprint became starkly visible even in the shadowed light the enormity of what she had done swept over her. Slow burning rage suffused his features and everything in her wanted to cower away from the hate that gleamed red in those piercing eyes, but she held her ground bravely, clenching her hands into fists by her side and standing straight as a ramrod.

'Have you quite finished?' The words were ground out through clenched teeth and she felt suddenly deflated and horribly alone.

'You deserved that,' she said fiercely, her eyes brimming with unshed tears.

'I did?' There was a note of genuine amazement in his voice, coupled with raw anger. 'You astound me.' He took a step towards her and caught the hand that had delivered the blow, spreading out the long pale fingers against his palm. He raised her hand slowly to his lips, gently kissing each finger in turn while his eyes never left her white face.

She stared at him silently, totally intimidated by the leashed power his gentleness accentuated.

His smile was faintly cruel. 'If you should ever think of repeating that little performance I will make you wish you had never been born.' The words were utterly devoid of feeling, which made them all the more chilling, and she snatched her hand away quickly with a little gasp of fright.

'I hate you.'

'So you've told me before.' Suddenly the icy eyes were glowing with constrained anger and some other emotion Ria couldn't define. 'That's fine, just keep it that way.' He strode into the taverna, returning almost immediately and roughly grabbing her arm, almost carrying her to the waiting car. He opened the door and hurled her into the padded seat, slamming the door and stalking round to the driver's side in seconds.

'Just sit still and don't say a word. I don't want to talk to you, I don't want to look at you.' His Greek accent was very pronounced.

The rest of the short journey was completed in deafening silence. Ria was by now past feeling anything except dreadfully ill. The combination of practically no sleep in the last forty-eight hours, the confrontation with Dimitrios and a nagging anxiety about Poppy had turned her nerve-endings into highly sensitised pinpoints of pain.

She sat huddled in her seat until Dimitrios swung the car off the road, past some large open white gates and drove up a short gravelled drive into a large paved area beyond which she could see the dim outline of an enormous white house. She was vaguely conscious of lights flashing on and illuminating the car in a rosy glow and dark figures moving towards them, but as she tried to get out of the car her trembling legs gave way and blackness was sweeping over her head in consuming waves.

'Come on, no more play-acting.' Dimitrios's rough voice sounded in her ear as he jostled her arm, but she was beyond speech, swimming in and out of consciousness as her head buzzed with a thousand images.

She was aware of a woman's voice, very loud, giving orders in an incomprehensible tongue, of a gentle hand being placed on her burning forehead and snatched sharply away, and of being carried into the bright lights that burnt against her closed eyelids. Then there was a cool darkness that smelt of something nice, the noise and commotion melted away and she lay still, cocooned in softness, slipping instantly into a deep dreamless sleep.

Ria awoke in a large bright room filled with clean white sunlight to what sounded like a hundred dogs barking somewhere below her. A soft warm breeze was ruffling white lace curtains in a gentle dance, and the heady perfume of summer was streaming in through the large open full-length windows. She moved her head drowsily on the pillows, bewildered by the strange room and confused, half-forgotten images in her mind.

'You are feeling better?' The low voice was soft with just the slightest inflexion of an accent. 'Don't be frightened.' Ria turned her head and the middle-aged woman who had been sitting in a large cane chair by her side smiled warmly and took her limp hand.

'Where am I?' Ria struggled to sit up but sank back on the soft silk pillows gratefully as a feeling of weakness overcame her. She was vaguely aware that her whole flat would easily fit into this vast, beautifully furnished bedroom. Dimitrios was indelibly printed on each imposing line.

A large porcelain statuette of a slim girl in Grecian dress with a garland of flowers in her long hair caught her attention. It was placed to one side of the open windows and the soft fine lace of the billowing curtains stroked the pale matt form caressingly, bringing a sudden vivid recollection of large brown hands gently touching her body.

'You are very welcome to our home, my dear; I have been longing to meet you.' The welcome was unaffectedly genuine.

'You are Christina?' Ria stammered a little. The warm, smiling woman at her side had none of the angry aggressiveness and proud arrogance that was so characteristic of her fiery brother. Gentle blue eyes glowed softly as Christina nodded slowly, seeming the only living things in the pale gaunt face. Dimitrios hadn't exaggerated, sickness had ravaged the thin body before her, grooving lines of pain into the strong features in which some vestige of beauty still remained.

'You were exhausted, my dear.' Christina deftly plumped the pillows as she spoke. 'The doctor said sleep was the best remedy and it appears he was right as usual.'

'How long have I been asleep?' Ria asked faintly, becoming aware that she was clothed only in the flimsiest of her nighties, lying between thin sheets in the biggest bed she had ever seen.

'Dimitrios brought you here nearly thirty-six hours ago.' The soft voice hardened fractionally. 'How my usually astute and sensible brother could ignore all the warning signs of extreme exhaustion is quite beyond me. What had you been doing to yourself?'

'Working too hard.' Ria hoped she wouldn't press for details.

'Did you tell Dimitrios how you felt?' The blue gaze became uncomfortably penetrating and for the first time the resemblance between brother and sister was obvious. As though the thought of him had conjured up his appearance the heavy oak door of the bedroom was flung open, saving Ria the necessity of replying, and an immediate uproar filled the room as a cascade of barking dogs descended in a great deluge towards the bed, causing Christina to rise in protest.

In the ensuing crescendo of sound she counted three tiny Yorkshire terriers who took it upon themselves to wash her face enthusiastically with very small pink tongues, two springer spaniels, a comical-faced little dog of indeterminate breed who kept up an ardent and vigorous assault on everyones hearing, and a beautiful sleek red setter that positioned itself gracefully at the side of the bed, lifting a welcoming paw. Two enormous Old English sheepdogs stood majestically in the centre of the room, shaggily silent, the tall commanding figure of their master behind them.

'Dimitrios! Get the dogs out of here,' Christina shouted into the mêlée, the pitch of her voice belying her frail form and causing the dogs to become still as though by magic, the whole pack turning ingratiatingly mournful eyes in her direction.

Ria pulled the sheets more firmly under her chin as the dogs slunk down, every pore in her body aware of Dimitrios's presence. Almost against her will her eyes were drawn upwards and as she met the steel-blue gaze a shiver of apprehension sent tiny shock waves down her spine. Oh, help, she thought frantically, why did he have to be so devastatingly handsome? The light-coloured feminine room made his dark maleness even more threatening, and she felt a tentacle of panic wrap itself round her body. He was going to be so angry when he found out the truth, if he didn't know already.

'Good morning.' The deep voice was as she remembered, cold and faintly quizzical. 'You are recovered?'

'Yes, thank you.' Ria forced her glance

away, feeling an almost physical wrench as her eyes left his. 'I'm sorry I have inconvenienced you,' she added stiffly. 'I can't remember much about the last day or so.'

'Really?' The words were heavy with meaning. 'You remember the journey from the airport, surely? We took some refreshment.' The unmistakable sarcasm brought her head up sharply and as she met his cool, bland gaze her cheeks burned with humiliating colour. He was reminding her how easily he had overcome her resistance, how she had all but proved to him that she was exactly what he had suspected. Her palm burnt with the sensation of flesh hitting flesh and she remembered with horror that she had actually dared to strike this autocratic block of ice.

'No? Doesn't ring any bells? Funny, you seemed quite lucid at that point.' He was watching her face intently, her thoughts mirrored in unconscious candour in her large grey eyes, and as she burned with self-contempt he seemed to suddenly tire of the game.

'Well, don't worry about it,' he said slowly as she let the heavy swing of silver hair hide her flushed face. 'The journey has faded into something of a blur for me too.'

Ria stole a glance at him from under her thick lashes. How can I hate you so much and feel so attracted at the same time? she thought wretchedly, hating her weakness. Perhaps he was going to let bygones be bygones after all. She didn't know what had changed his mind but was grateful for a reprieve from the veiled taunts.

Christina looked from her brother's rugged face to the young slim girl in the huge bed, sensing the tight atmosphere between them and at a loss to understand it.

Just then a timid knock sounded at the half-open door and a small elderly woman entered carrying a large tray holding hot rolls, various kinds of preserves, fresh orange juice and coffee. 'This is our housekeeper, Rosa.' Christina nodded at Ria, and the little woman smiled briefly at her as she turned and scuttled away like a frightened rabbit.

'Dimitrios makes her nervous,' Christina explained apologetically, and as Ria caught his eye over Christina's head he smiled sardonically, and, with a wicked little salute in her direction, turned sharply, clicking his fingers at the dogs who immediately followed.

'How strange,' Ria replied with wry humour, wondering if all Greek men were going to have such a catastrophic effect on her nervous system. Christina flashed her another searching glance as she moved with her brother to the door, leaning heavily on a carved ebony walking stick.

'I'll see you later, my dear,' she said graciously as she left the room slowly. 'Please look upon this house as your home and we will make every effort to ensure you enjoy your stay with us.'

Dimitrios paused in the doorway, and as they heard Christina's slow steps moving away down the hall he moved swiftly back into the room, picking up the loaded tray from the small table where the housekeeper had laid it, and placing it across her lap as she huddled into the sheets. He noticed her shrinking withdrawal at his approach and smiled coldly, satisfaction glowing in the dark blue depths of his eyes.

'You are in my territory now, my little English rose,' he said grimly, his face proud and still. 'You will play by my rules here. If you behave yourself you may indeed have a pleasant stay in my beautiful country; if not...' He shrugged, heavy lids covering the cruel gleam that momentarily sprang into his eyes.

Ria stared at him in fascinated horror as he turned away. 'I can be a kind, even considerate master,' he said mockingly over his shoulder as be left the room, 'and I'm sure somewhere in that little feline brain of yours there is a secret wish to be subdued, even perhaps conquered—who knows?' He filled the doorway with black energy as he stood, his narrowed gaze raking her white face, his muscled body powerful and controlled. 'I think I can promise you an interesting stay whatever the outcome.' He smiled slowly and shut the door with exaggerated care, leaving her trembling and shaken in the sure knowledge that she had inadvertently walked into the King of the Beasts' lair.

CHAPTER THREE

Left alone, Ria found she was surprisingly hungry, and demolished the contents of the tray ravenously. Replete, she took stock of her surroundings, padding across the thick cream carpet to find a small ornate bathroom hidden behind a smooth sliding door, the other side of which was a huge walk-in wardrobe where her few clothes hung in solitary splendour.

Moving over to the windows, she brushed the lace aside and stepped on to the small balcony beyond, catching her breath in wonderment. A magical paradise was spread out before her in panoramic splendour, the house being built on the top of a gently sloping cliff that led down to a small picturesque harbour dozing in the hot sun. Far in the distance dazzling white houses clustered in small groups perched on sun-baked rocky slopes rising from a brilliantly gleaming turquoise sea which merged effortlessly with the clear blue sky overhead. To the left of the harbour Ria could see a steep circuitous track leading to a small sleepy village, along which a laden donkey was methodically picking its way in a manner that had remained unchanged for centuries.

'I can't believe this,' she murmured softly to herself, her bare feet soaking up the warmth from the hot marble tiles. She leaned over the mellow old stone to find a long tiered garden below, alive with riotous colour, sweetly perfumed shrubs, masses of exotic flowers and scattered fruit trees all competing for supremacy. Low wooden tables and chairs were dotted here and there under the shady trees, and immediately below several fat lazy cats in varying shapes and colours lay basking dreamily on a tiled veranda.

'Now that's what I call a view.' The lazy voice penetrated her stupor a second before the realisation that she was standing practically naked hit her. As she jerked violently back, a low, sardonic chuckle met her ears, and she just caught sight of the top of Dimitrios's dark head close to the stone wall that surrounded the garden. She fled into the bedroom, her heart giving a little kick as she remembered the scorn in that drawling voice. Everything she did seemed to confirm his opinion of her, she thought despairingly.

As she stood under the shower, the warm water stinging away the last remnants of sleep, her thoughts centred on Poppy and the desperation she had heard in her cousin's voice. Whatever had transpired between her cousin and Dimitrios's nephew, it had been no light affair. With a little lurch of dismay she remembered that she hadn't even spoken Nikos's name to Christina. Hardly the picture of a loving fiancée.

'I just can't win,' she muttered bleakly to the tiled wall in front of her, washing her hair in the deliciously perfumed shampoo she had found in the bathroom and wrapping herself in one of the huge fluffy towels before sitting on the balcony, her face upturned to the sun's rays. Her long thick hair was spread out like spun silver over her shoulders to dry, its silky sheen reflecting the sunlight, and the hot still air was heavy with a hundred different scents.

She shut her eyes against the sun's glare, relaxing in this safe little oasis in a hostile world.

The ominously threatening shadow was close behind her, relentless and cold. She mustn't face it, she had to keep moving, but her feet were too heavy to move and this vile thing had her in its power. It was going to catch her, it was reaching out—Ria awoke from the nightmare hot and shaken, the images so vivid in her mind that she gave a scream of pure terror when a dark shape moved at the side of her.

'It's all right.' Dimitrios's voice was quiet and soothing. 'You were having a bad dream, that's all. You're quite safe.' Ria raised dazed soft eyes to his face and caught a strange look in his unguarded eyes moments before a shutter came down and his expression resumed its normal cynical façade. That look frightened her more than the dream; it was raw hunger and something else she had never seen on another human's face, a kind of bitter haunted yearning.

'Do you usually display yourself to all and sundry while you take the air?' He leant his long lean shape casually against the edge of the balcony, looking out over the harbour. As the daylight dispelled the last remnants of the dream Ria rose shakily to her feet, clasping the towel tightly to her body.

'I wasn't displaying myself and there is no one around anyway,' she retorted defiantly to his broad back, and he turned sharply, his eyes shooting blue sparks.

'What am I? A figment of your imagination?' he asked sarcastically, his eyes slowly peeling the towel from her body until she felt naked, hot colour flooding her pale skin.

'You don't count!' she shot back furiously, incensed at his autocratic behaviour, and had the momentary satisfaction of seeing his taunting expression freeze in surprise. A small muscle twitched warningly in his smooth tanned cheek as he moved lazily towards her.

'I don't, eh?' His voice was deceptively soft. 'Shall we put that to the test?' She tried to move away a fraction too late, his hands catching her slender wrists in an iron grip that was bruisingly harsh. He pulled her close to his body and as she twisted in his grasp she felt the towel begin to slip and immediately froze, bitterly regretting her words and the cold anger they had aroused. He towered over her, his big shoulders shutting out the sun and his face as black as thunder.

'I warned you before to keep those

little claws sheathed, didn't I?' he said grimly, shaking her slightly like a dog with a bone.

'Don't, you're hurting me,' Ria whispered indistinctly, his proximity doing crazy things to her insides. She felt the towel slide a little further and the smooth material of his shirt rubbed against one full bare breast, sending a little shiver of desire down her spine. 'Please, Dimitrios...'

'You wanted this, didn't you? Knew I'd come to find you?' His voice was thick and accusing. 'I told you you can't play your games with me.' As the towel slipped down to rest on her hips his eyes burnt down her body and it felt as though he was already touching each curve and contour.

He suddenly pushed her to arm's length, still holding on to her wrists but pulling her arms up slightly so that her breasts were lifted to his hot gaze. 'Let's have a good look at what's being offered.' As the cold hard words reached her she felt a humiliation so deep that she wished she could die. To have to stand before him like this...

Her eyes were blind with embarrassment, all colour leaving her face, and as his eyes swept up to her face his expression altered suddenly when he saw her distress.

'Don't look like that!' He swore softly and vehemently as he jerked her close into his body, pulling the towel protectively round her trembling shoulders, his hands not quite steady.

They stood quite still for a moment and she could feel his heartbeat racing madly, his breathing erratic. 'What kind of animal are you turning me into?' he murmured into her fragrant hair, and she jerked convulsively in his hold, wrenching herself away as a small sob broke in her throat.

'I didn't do anything. It was you, it's always you. You won't leave me alone.' Her expression was wild. 'The dream was all your fault too.' She sank down on the sun warmed seat hugging the towel to her as he stared at her in amazement.

'I should be used to the way a woman's brain works by now, but you've lost me this time,' he said slowly, moving away from her, his hands gripping the edge of the balcony until his knuckles were white against the mellow stone. 'How on earth have you made me responsible for that nightmare?'

'I haven't had that dream in years

until you made me come here,' Ria said tremulously, suddenly aware that she was on dangerous ground. The less she said, the better.

'You used to have the dream often?' Dimitrios questioned, turning and holding her eyes in a keen probing stare. 'Why? There must have been a trigger for a young girl to consistently experience something like that.'

Ria broke his hypnotic gaze with difficulty, bending her head and letting her hair become a silver veil. 'I had a trigger, yes,' she affirmed quietly, her voice dismissive, rising to enter the bedroom.

Dimitrios's harsh voice cut through the air like a sharp knife. 'Sit down, please. We will discuss this further.'

'I can't.' Unable to stand another physical confrontation and feeling at a distinct disadvantage, Ria grasped the back of the chair with nerveless fingers. How could she explain that her family's violent death had haunted her sleep for years? As far as Dimitrios was aware her father was alive. 'Please, Dimitrios, I really can't.'

'You can. I intend to know what makes you tick, Poppy. It's almost as though you have a split personality, and I want to know why.' His face was unrelenting.

'I need to go in the shade. The sun is too hot and it's making me dizzy.' As his magnetic eyes travelled over her flushed skin she shivered suddenly in spite of the fierce heat. 'Please.'

He stared for one long moment at her troubled face and then took her arm gently, leading her into the cool air-conditioned bedroom where the faint perfume of fresh flowers from a beautifully arranged bowl of tiny blooms scented the air.

'I forgot the English skin is so thin and you have been unwell. I would suggest you have a siesta after lunch which I will ask Rosa to bring to you here, and then you will be fresh enough to join us downstairs for dinner at eight.' He walked slowly to the door as he spoke, turning with his hand on the handle, his glance searching. 'You won't always be able to evade my questions so easily, young lady. I need some answers and I need them fast; I'm not a patient man.' She lowered her eyelids at his tight scrutiny, turning her face away, her fingers running distractedly over the smooth porcelain of the graceful statuette.

'You could have modelled for that.' As

she raised startled eyes to his she saw a deep slumbrous heat in the blue depths. 'White, cool and untouched, or wanton and cruel. Oh, we are definitely going to have to have a talk very soon.' He shut the door quietly as he spoke, leaving her trembling and shaken. There had been a cold threat in those last words.

After eating her light but delicious lunch of cold meat and salad followed by a lemon mousse whipped to a tangy cream foam, Ria dressed quickly in a long flowered skirt and simple white top. Her mind was too active for her to sleep again, and, stopping only to brush her silver-gilt hair into a silky ponytail, her face clear of make-up, she decided to explore.

As she left her room the sheer size of the villa overwhelmed her. A magnificent highly polished staircase curved seemingly endlessly from the wide sunlit landing, sweeping into a huge room that stretched the whole length of the house. Beautifully painted vases as tall as herself lined one white wall, each one holding a different type of fern so the whole wall was a mass of delicate green patterns moving gently in the slight breeze from the open windows.

At the far end of the room large french

windows opened on to the garden where the cats were still spread out in the afternoon sun, their tails twitching lazily at her approach.

'I thought you would ignore my suggestion of a siesta.' As she stepped into the sunshine she saw Dimitrios, clad only in a pair of light shorts, his bronzed muscular body exposed to the sun, lying in the shade of some orange trees, the inevitable dogs spread out round his feet like a canine carpet.

She stood transfixed in the doorway, breathtakingly aware of his lean, powerful physique gleaming in the sun, the black body hair curling thickly on his broad chest and disappearing down the hard flat stomach where a single jagged scar stood out vividly white against the bronzed skin.

'A memento of my wild youth,' he said briefly, following her eyes. 'The lady forgot to mention she was married until her husband turned up with a twelve-inch knife.'

Ria stared at him, fascinated, and teasing, heavy-lidded eyes wandered over her flushed face. 'I'm afraid I'm a wicked man,' he drawled mockingly, amusement tinting the dark voice. 'It would seem we are two of a kind.'

Colour flooded her face and she tore her eyes away, stumbling over one of the sleeping cats as she made her way towards him, unable to dispel the sad ache his words had aroused. He rose at her approach, moving over to a nearby table and chairs on which a half-full bottle of light sparkling wine reposed beside two crystal glasses.

'Two glasses?' she questioned, glancing around curiously, and he smiled, showing strong white teeth.

'I told you, I knew you would be down sooner or later.' He poured her a glass of the effervescent liquid, his face tightening as she flinched when his fingers inadvertently touched hers.

'It's all right, I'm not going to ravish you here in my garden,' he said irritably, stretching back in his chair and shutting his eyes.

'I know.' Her voice came out high and squeaky and she cleared her throat nervously before trying again. 'I'm sorry.' The morning's events were still too vivid in her mind for her to relax in his presence, the humiliation too deep.

The brief nine months she had been a model on her arrival in London had been bad enough, but at least when she had modelled swimwear and endless skimpy cocktail dresses it had been necessary for her work and before strangers. She would always be grateful to Julian for making a way of escape from that particular horror. The blatant unconcealed lust in male eyes had caused her to withdraw even more into herself. That was why Julian had been such a blessing, she remembered fondly; his friendship had been totally without strings and blissfully platonic.

She glanced at Dimitrios under her eyelashes, annoyed at the effect his body was having on her when she had thought she was immune to men. 'You have a beautiful home,' she tried conversationally, relieved her voice was almost normal again.

'I'm most fortunate,' he agreed smoothly, opening his eyes lazily and meeting her timid gaze. 'If I didn't know better I would think you weren't used to being around a half-naked man.' The stark words made her jump.

The colour that had just subsided leapt into her face again, and he stretched out a big brown hand and stroked her warm cheek thoughtfully. 'I like that,' he said approvingly, his eyes for once losing the guarded expression that was habitual when he looked at her. 'I wasn't aware that women still knew how to blush.'

Ria stared in mute confusion, more angry with her own gaucherie than his goading, jerking her face away from his touch and making her ponytail swing.

'Is this part of the image?' The shutters were back in place in the cold face as he flicked her hair lightly.

'I don't know what you mean.'

'I see. You are unaware that you look about fifteen with your hair like that?' His voice was scathingly disbelieving. 'Virginal and untouched?'

'I did my hair like this because it's cooler,' she answered crossly. Even the way she did her hair was wrong! 'Anyway, who are you to judge whether I'm untouched or not?' Now why had she said that? she thought miserably; that was an invitation for more insults if ever she had heard one.

He didn't reply immediately, taking a sip of wine before he leant forward to hold her eyes tightly with his own. 'Poppy, Nikos was very upset when he came home the last time. He told me...things he wouldn't normally have revealed.'

'Yes?' she asked dully, knowing she wasn't going to like what she heard.

He sighed impatiently. 'You aren't making this very easy. Do I have to spell it out or will you do us both a favour and forget the pure and innocent routine? It's beginning to get on my nerves.'

Her slight shoulders stiffened at his insulting tone, but she couldn't quite meet his gaze. Her suspicions about Poppy would be clear for him to read. 'Tell me what he said.'

He swore softly and fluently under his breath. 'How did this conversation start anyway?'

'What did he say?' she persisted, her voice taut.

'Look, he was under some stress.' Dimitrios was clearly finding this distasteful. 'He explained that you had slept together and that although it was the first time for him you had been honest enough to confess you had had other lovers before him.'

The words dropped like tiny pieces of ice into Ria's heart.

'Why did you have to tell him you didn't

84

love the others, that he was the love of your life?' His voice was accusingly harsh. 'He was crazy enough about you to accept anything; why lead him on and agree to marry him if it was all just another farce?' His voice was throbbing with such strong emotion that Ria involuntarily raised her eyes to his, recoiling as the hate leapt out at her like a live thing. 'You broke him, Poppy, and heaven alone only knows where he is now.'

'He's not here?'

'Of course he's not here. Do you think we'd be sitting here like this if he were?'

'I didn't know,' she whispered quietly.

'You didn't ask.' The words were, totally condemning. 'I've been waiting since this morning for you to ask about him. You haven't even mentioned his name.'

'Didn't he say where he was going?' she asked dully, feeling as though she couldn't take any more. She would have to tell him the truth; everything was suddenly out of hand.

'Apparently just after I left for England he had an urgent telephone call from someone. He left almost immediately, leaving a message with Rosa for his mother to say he had a delicate business matter to attend to.'

'You don't believe him?' Ria asked nervously, sensing Dimitrios's hesitation.

'I neither believe nor disbelieve him,' he answered coldly. 'However, my nephew is not in the habit of telling lies, so I am sure there is an excellent explanation for his absence. He'll have the pleasure of finding you here on his return, won't he?'

'You don't think he'd do anything silly?' Ria's voice was trembling.

'You mean besides getting involved with you in the first place?' His voice was cutting. 'Of course not. Nikos is a Greek.' As far as be was concerned that said it all.

'He did know you were coming to fetch me?' Ria asked slowly, a certain inflexion in the cool voice feeding the growing suspicion in her mind.

'Not exactly.' The narrowed eyes dared her to object. 'I am the head of this house and the occupants are my responsibility. My nephew is still young and somewhat emotional. It was necessary to be firm with him to avoid Christina being upset.'

'Nikos didn't ask for me to come?'

'I asked you to come.' The thread of steel running through the harsh voice warned Ria to be careful. 'That is sufficient. Once Nikos sees you here in his home environment he will understand the unsuitability of any...friendship between you, and after a few weeks I shall take Christina on a long cruise to regain her strength. On our return you will be gone and Nikos will inform his mother that the matter was settled amicably.'

Ria felt a flame of anger leap through her; his cool effrontery grated on her raw nerves. 'Just a minute,' she said tersely, her slender body rigid and straight. 'What gives you the right to make all these plans, to judge what's right for us all?'

'Not all,' he replied quietly, his voice calm. 'Just my family. You are of no importance.'

The unemotional words hurt more than she would ever have thought possible. Dimitrios watched her with indifferent eyes, his big body motionlessly relaxed. In spite of outward appearances she had the feeling he was waiting to pounce at the first opportunity, a relentless jungle cat stalking its prey.

An overwhelming desire to challenge his cold authority swept over her and she rose slowly, her face stiff with pain.

'The great illustrious Dimitrios,' she bit out grimly, 'so right, so perfect, so far above the rest of us poor simple mortals. Do you know something? I pity you, I really do. You're nothing but a dried up shell.'

'That's enough.'

Ria failed to detect the ultimatum in the mild tone. 'All this righteous disapproval! You make me sick. At least Nikos can feel love, which is more than you can. You're incapable of normal emotion. I bet you've never really loved anyone in your life—'

Whatever else she might have said was abruptly cut off as he stood up, pulling her to him in one fluid motion, clamping his hand tightly across her mouth until she felt her neck would snap.

'Be quiet,' he ground out through clenched teeth, his face a livid mask of fury. 'You dare to criticise me! A little tramp like you talking of love. You are most fortunate Christina is upstairs resting or I'd whip you to within an inch of your life.'

She struggled in his grasp and he moved his hand from her mouth, looking down at her with angry eyes. 'It was a mistake to bring you here; you are nothing but trouble.'

'I didn't want to come,' she flung back hotly, trembling in his hold.

'But you are here, aren't you?' he said softly, a subtle change entering his face. 'And we'll just have to make the best of it.' As she looked at him she could almost see the armour being put back into place, the distant coldness clothing his frame and the cruel cynical mask settling over his features.

'You're experienced enough to know the effect you have on me—' his voice was slightly husky and she could feel the stirring in his body as he pressed her softness against him '—but don't be fooled by that. It's pure old-fashioned lust, my dear. I want your body, no more, no less.' He smiled coldly, his eyes hard. 'It's quite possible for a man to take a woman's comfort while despising the giver.'

Her legs were shaking so much that she could hardly stand. The feel of his body against hers was frightening but exciting. This side of life was quite unknown to her, and his maleness was overpowering.

'Women like you disgust me, but I would be the first to admit you are not in the usual mould.' His voice had become quite bland even as his body moved against hers, and as she wrenched herself from his hold he smiled again. 'Just be careful.'

He left without another word and she sat in the shade of the trees for a long time, the gentle company of the animals soothing the wounds his words inflicted. Several small lizards, jade-green against the lichened stone of the old wall, popped out to take a fleeting look at the intruder in their domain before they darted back to their hiding place. Overhead a solitary plane droned its toneless melody in the fierce heat and as the dogs moved in a protective heap around her body, settling back into their twitching slumber, she felt her eyelids grow heavy. No one came to find her and after a while she slept, waking a good deal later to find dusk creeping into the garden, its long shadowed fingers causing the tiny birds to chatter their goodnights noisily overhead. The rest had revived her mind and calmed her spirit, her thoughts crystallised in slumber. 'I must tell him the truth,' she said softly into the night, a dart of pain searing her heart. 'I must get away.' She didn't try to analyse why.

Later, as she sat putting the last touches to her make-up before going down to dinner, there was a light tap at the bedroom door and her heart jumped nervously. 'Come in.'

To her relief Christina's gentle face appeared round the door, the thin body stooping as she made her way over to where Ria sat in front of the long marble dressing-table.

'I'm sorry I haven't been a good hostess, my dear.' The soft voice was apologetic. 'I'm afraid it's a case of the mind being willing but the flesh weak.'

'That's all right,' Ria replied warmly, fetching the easy-chair from the side of the bed and helping Christina to sit. 'I don't expect you to entertain me.'

'Has Dimitrios been looking after you?' The words were casual but the soft blue eyes were tight on her face, and Ria couldn't stop the tell-tale pink colour flooding her pale cheeks.

Christina leant forward before she could reply, the lined face earnest. 'My dear, I feel there are a few things about our family I should explain to you before any misunderstandings are allowed to develop. I don't normally discuss our private affairs and I would ask you to be patient with me if I ramble on a little.'

'Please, there is no need—' Ria began, but Christina stopped her with a small sorrowful shake of her head.

'You will understand.' She settled back in the chair, her breathing a little laboured. 'I couldn't help but notice that you seem on edge with my brother, Poppy; his attitude towards you is perhaps a trifle hostile?' Ria looked at the older woman in concern—how much had those perceptive, knowing eyes seen?

'To understand Dimitrios and—how do you English say it?—what makes him tick,' she smiled briefly, 'I must go back quite a few years in our history. Our mother was English; you have perhaps noticed that English is as natural to us as Greek?'

Ria nodded. It also explained the vivid blue eyes.

'Our mother died giving birth to Dimitrios when I was a newly married bride of twenty. Since I had been born she had suffered numerous miscarriages and difficulties but our father demanded a son and so she persevered against all medical advice.' Christina's expression hardened. 'My father was a very arrogant man.'

'A nanny was hired for the baby but the arrangement proved unsatisfactory and when my father was killed in a riding accident when Dimitrios was nine months old my husband and I took him into our home to bring up as our own. It was my brother's birthright to grow up in his father's home so we sold our house and moved here.' She stopped for a moment and twisted the thick gold band on her left hand. 'My husband was a good man.

'For many years it looked as though Dimitrios would be our only family; I had inherited my mother's problems, you understand. But when Dimitrios was fifteen Nikos was born. They were wonderful years.' Her thin face glowed with distant memories and Ria caught a glimpse of the young Christina, happy, fulfilled and in love.

'My mother had a younger sister in England whose daughter was the same age as Dimitrios, and one summer when Nikos was seven she came to stay with us. She got on very well with Dimitrios.' Her voice shook as she continued, 'I shall always blame myself that I didn't realise just how well. Andreas—my husband—and I were heavily committed to the family business and Nikos was quite demanding at that time, but I should have known what was happening. One evening Andreas and I returned home unexpectedly and found them—how can I say?—they were as man and wife.'

Ria felt as though she had been punched hard in the stomach, searing hot jealousy attacking her for the first time in her life. What's the matter with me? she thought in horror. Of course he's had women in the past. Lots of them, he's all but told me. He means nothing to me. But a little cold voice in some untouched part of her brain wouldn't let her fool herself any longer. You love him, it whispered stealthily, you love him.

'It was a great shock to my husband,' Christina was continuing, unaware of Ria's distress. 'It is not right for such a thing to happen before marriage, and with his cousin, a guest in our home entrusted to our care! Andreas was deeply upset.'

Christina paused and wiped some moistre from her lips; the story was obviously taking its toll.

'Dimitrios loved Caroline very much and asked her to marry him immediately.' Ria's stomach twisted. 'She looked at him and laughed; in front of all of us she laughed.' The older woman winced at the memory, her eyes looking back down the years. 'She told us she was already engaged to a boy in England at the university she attended. Dimitrios was just a pleasant way to pass the summer, a dalliance.'

She turned to Ria, taking her hand and pressing it between her own. 'You must understand, in Greece girls do not go with a man before marriage, only a certain sort of girl behaves that way. For a young girl of good family to act as Caroline did was a total enigma to Dimitrios. He had supposed she felt as he did; he was young and very naïve.'

Ria took a deep breath. Where was all this leading?

'Caroline was sent home in disgrace. Three days later my husband suffered a massive heart attack and died in my arms.' She turned pain-filled eyes to Ria's white face. 'Dimitrios blamed himself, maybe he still does. The postmortem revealed Andreas had been living on borrowed time for years, but Dimitrios wouldn't accept that. He insisted the shock of finding Caroline with him that way had killed Andreas.'

Christina stood up slowly, leaning heavily on the marble top of the dressing-table.

'The thing is, Poppy, your likeness to Caroline is remarkable.' Ria stared at her in horror.

'She had your unusual colour of hair and slim build. Admittedly her eyes were blue and she was a little taller than you, but you could be sisters. The first time I saw you it was quite a shock.'

So that was it—she hadn't stood a chance. From the first moment he had seen her he had been punishing her for the old tragedy enacted all those years ago. He looked at her and saw Caroline, and the way Poppy had treated Nikos had fuelled the fire.

'Please try and understand,' Christina said pleadingly, seeing her white face. 'I don't want things spoilt for you and my son, and I'm sure once Dimitrios gets to know you he will realise you are quite different from Caroline. It's just a little hard for him to adjust; he is a man of very deep feelings.'

'Yes, I see,' Ria said dazedly, her mind trying to absorb all she had been told. Christina patted her shoulder gently and just for a moment Ria was tempted to tell her the truth, but some little demon of fear held her back and the moment was lost. It would be confirmation to Dimitrios that she was all he had suspected when he found out she had deceived him, made him look a fool for the second time. If he hated her now what would he feel then? Her body shrank in terror. She had to get away, to escape before he found out the truth.

'But I love him,' she said into the empty room, Christina having left, quietly closing the door behind her. 'How can I love him when he hates me?' The silent room gave her no answer and she sat staring at her reflection in the mirror, wishing with all her heart that she had been born plain and ugly, tears running in a torrent down her white cheeks.

CHAPTER FOUR

Dinner was a stilted affair. There were just the three of them sitting at the huge polished table, all lost in their own thoughts. Ria could only pick at the delicious food, the lump in her throat threatening to choke her with each mouthful.

'You aren't on some sort of diet, are you?' Dimitrios asked disapprovingly. 'I know you models have to stay slim but you'll melt away completely at this rate.' His eyes swept dispargingly over her slender frame.

'Dimitrios!' Christina's sharp eyes had caught his look and Ria's blushes.

'No, I'm just not hungry,' Ria said hastily into the charged atmosphere. 'The food is lovely, though.' It was. Rosa was obviously an excellent cook. After slices of fresh fruit marinated in wine and honey, the housekeeper had produced a wonderful rice dish bursting with juicy prawns, crab and other seafood, served with thin slices of brown bread flavoured with garlic. A fresh green salad and small potato balls rolled in a coating of herbs and breadcrumbs was next with succulent slices of veal in a rich creamy sauce.

At the little housekeeper's hurt look at her constant refusal, Ria forced down a small helping of the sticky honey pudding, full of nuts and cream, gulping at the deep red fruity wine to ease it past the ache in her throat.

'We'll have coffee in the garden, please, Rosa,' Christina instructed as they finished the meal, rising with Dimitrios's help and walking slowly into the scented darkness, leaning heavily on her brother's arm. Ria followed uncertainly, her new perception noticing how gently Dimitrios's big hands settled Christina into an easy-chair, pulling a light rug across her lap tenderly, his face warm with love. Suddenly she couldn't face an evening of polite conversation with his eyes and ears trained on her every move.

'Would you mind if I had an early night?' she apologised to Christina. 'I have a headache.' It was quite true, the day's events had combined to produce a painful throbbing in the back of her head and her eyes ached with the effort of keeping them open.

'Not at all,' Christina began, concern darkening her eyes, but Dimitrios interrupted smoothly, his gaze faintly threatening over his sister's head.

'A cup of coffee is just what you need, then, and the fresh air will work wonders on that headache.' It was obvious he didn't believe her, little blue darts gleaming in his dark gaze. 'My sister informs me I have been neglecting my duties as host,' he continued as she still hesitated in the doorway of the house. 'She suggests we could do a little sight-seeing tomorrow if you feel up to it.' His face was wickedly mocking; he knew exactly how she felt about the suggestion.

She groaned inwardly, understanding Christina's attempt at kindness with a sinking heart. How could she know that Dimitrios's company was a subtle torture to her?

'That would be lovely,' she said weakly, conceding defeat and sitting down miserably by Christina's side. She was vitally aware of Dimitrios's hawklike presence to the right of her, his white open-necked shirt revealing his powerful bronzed chest, the casual light grey trousers moulded to his body like a second skin. She wouldn't have been surprised if the air had suddenly crackled around them.

They made casual small talk for about an hour until Christina stood up to leave, her face drawn and tired in the dull light. 'No, no,' she objected as Ria repeated her plea for an early night. 'Stay and talk to Dimitrios for a while. You two should get to know each other.' She smiled conspiratorially at Ria as she left, quite oblivious to the panic in her face.

'What would you like to see tomorrow?' He relaxed as his sister left, stretching out his long legs in front of him and crossing his arms behind his neck as he lay back in his seat. His expression was indiscernible in the shadowed light but she had the uncomfortable impression he was playing with her like a cat with a mouse.

'I don't mind,' she said simply, her eyes searching out his face in the blackness.

'How very submissive,' the dry voice intoned mockingly. 'Have you perhaps decided to stop fighting me after all?'

Her eyes blurred as she took a deep breath, the knowledge she had gained about the cold proud man before her causing a little break in her voice as she replied, 'I'd like us to be friends.'

'Just friends?' His voice was suspicious, as if detecting another trick.

'Just friends.' The sincerity in her voice must have got through to him, because he leant forward suddenly, taking her small chin in his hands and forcing her head up to look deep into the soft grey eyes.

'Well, how about that? I think perhaps you really mean it.'

'I do.' She nodded as she assured him, her loose blonde hair trailing silkily over his hand. He caught a tendril as it fell back against her shoulders, looking at the fine gilt with a brooding expression on the handsome face.

'You don't see many people with this colour of hair,' he said almost to himself, 'like moonlight in the darkness.'

'My mother had it.' She spoke without thinking, the magic of his closeness making her incautious. 'My brother too.'

'Your brother?' He sprang immediately. 'Nikos didn't tell me you had a brother.'

'He's dead.' The words were stark. It was the first time she had ever mentioned Simon to anyone other than Poppy. 'He died when he was a baby.'

'I'm sorry. An accident?' Dimitrios said softly, watching the dead expression on her face closely.

'Yes. My mother died with him. He was twelve months old.'

'And you were?'

'I was seven.'

There was complete silence except for the distant high-pitched croaking of an insect somewhere in the undergrowth.

'That would have been very hard for you.' It was the first time he had ever used that tender tone with her, although she had heard it when he spoke to Christina many times. It was nearly her undoing. She had the strangest longing to put her head on the table and wail like a child.

'Did your father resent coping with a young child all by himself? Is that the cause of the rift between you?'

She hesitated, cold reason washing over her like an icy flood. He saw the change in her face and his own hardened in response. 'Well?' The word was clipped.

'I don't want to discuss it.' She moved to turn away but he caught hold of her arm in a gentle but firm grip.

'Not this time, Poppy. I want some answers this time.'

'I can't give you any answers.' The desperation in her voice got through to him and he stared at her with narrowed eyes.

'Why? Because you don't like me personally, or can't you talk to anyone?'

His eyes seemed to bore into her, black in the moonlight and oddly compelling. He looked unbelievably handsome.

'What about you?' Unconsciously she had decided attack was the best defence, primitive instincts of survival coming to the fore.

'Me? We aren't discussing me,' he said in surprise, his voice cold.

'Well, perhaps we should,' she answered recklessly, ignoring the warning tightening in his mouth. 'Why are you so hostile all the time? What's made you the way you are?'

'That's enough.' He stood up swiftly, walking towards the house. 'I congratulate you,' he said over his shoulder as he disappeared through the french windows. 'Once again you have engineered your own way. The conversation is at an end.'

Alone in her room she undressed swiftly, climbing thankfully between the cool soft sheets and burying her head in her arms.

How could her life have been altered so dramatically in the space of a few days? Was this feeling she felt for him love? Did love rip you apart with nonchalant ease and cast you into chasms of unutterable despair? 'I can't stand it,' she muttered into her pillow as hot tears stung their way through her closed eyelids, beginning to sob helplessly as desolation washed over her in great waves. She was unaware of the light knock at her door an hour later, having sank into exhausted sleep, smooth slim arms flung over her silver head, a single shining tear caught on her long dark lashes.

She stirred slightly as the big figure standing looking down at her brushed the teardrop on to his finger with a deep sigh, his face hidden in the darkness, and when after an age he left the room she moved restlessly in the vast bed before relaxing back into tired slumber.

An old church bell woke her early the next morning, its mellow tones calling the faithful to early prayer, and she lay dreamily in the mauve shadows, the house quiet and still around her. Someone had opened the balcony door as she slept and a cool, slightly salty breeze blew refreshingly on her sleepy face.

She suddenly longed to be outside in the fresh morning air, and after dressing swiftly in crisp white trousers and a warm jumper, as the morning was still quite cool, she brushed her hair till it shone like molten silver and quietly crept downstairs.

The dogs were nowhere to be seen, and she stood quite still in the deserted garden for a time, drinking in the smell and the feel of the foreign land as the birds chorused the dawn and the sky turned a mass of soft pinks and mauves. The heavy sweet perfume of trailing honeysuckle and jasmine from the old stone wall filled her nostrils with its intoxicating scent, and purple hibiscus and bright pink oleanders vied with tubs of vermilion and scarlet geraniums to greet the brilliant sunshine that was banishing the soft dawn.

Far in the distance the bob of tiny boats heralded the return of the small fishing-fleet loaded with the night's catch, and she stood idly watching them for a time, her eyes turning inwards towards the deep ache in her chest that wouldn't go away.

'Peaceful, isn't it?' The laconic deep voice brought her head up sharply and she turned to where Dimitrios was standing by an open wooden gate halfway down the long garden. He gestured to the two enormous wicker baskets at his feet. 'Successful night.'

'You've been fishing?' Ria couldn't keep the surprise out of her voice. His stained clothes and gleaming salty skin demonstrated he had been more than a casual observer. It was the first time she had ever seen him anything but immaculate, and if possible he looked even more attractive as he gazed at her with his normal inscrutable expression, the dogs bounding madly between them. At a sharp click from his fingers they subsided in a subdued heap under the trees, paws outstretched and tongues lolling.

'You find that surprising?' He was laughing at her again. 'I also eat, sleep and do other things that normal men do.' His eyes were wicked.

She lowered her head quickly but not before he had seen the inevitable pink response to his teasing. 'I don't consider being a member of a fishing-fleet "normal",' she said stiffly and heard his light laugh in reply.

'It is round here,' he said, his voice

serious now. 'How else do you think most men support their families? The sea is both friend and master.'

'Do you own a boat?' Ria asked as he lifted the loaded baskets on to his back, his muscled body tensing under the weight.

'I own the fleet,' he replied shortly, and, seeing her amazement, continued, 'My paternal grandfather built a large processing factory in Koista many years ago. It proved a wise investment and the business developed rapidly. When my father inherited the business he invested money in many different avenues; he was a shrewd businessman, I understand.' The hard face was expressionless. 'Most of the profit now comes from other areas but the factories hold their own and give the people a pride in their living. That is vitally important for such a small, close-knit community.'

'Yes, I suppose so.' It looked as though the Koutsoupis family was wealthier than she had ever imagined.

'I don't intend that my children will forget their roots.' It was as though he could read her mind.

'Your children?' asked Ria weakly, her heart thudding, and he smiled slowly.

'I was talking metaphorically,' he said softly. 'There are no little Dimitrioses yet. Unless you'd like to remedy that state of affairs?' He walked up the garden as he spoke, bent almost double under the weight of the loaded baskets. 'Ask Rosa to bring some coffee and rolls out here now, would you? I'm too hungry to shower first. Please join me if you haven't already eaten.'

He disappeared into a small alcove to one side of the house where the huge deep-freezers were kept. Christina had explained the previous evening that most of their supplies were delivered quarterly, making them quite self-sufficient on a day-to-day basis.

By the time he returned breakfast was waiting, and as they sipped the hot sweet coffee and ate the warm soft rolls Ria reflected that they could have been one of a thousand young married couples enjoying some time together before the day's events began. Heat was already hazing the distant mountains where the tiny dotted houses were becoming visible, the sun rising in the clear azure air like a ball of fire. A slight breeze ruffled Ria's pale hair, causing it to shimmer like silk in the clear light. It was going to be a beautiful day. She sighed heavily.

'Sounds as if you could have done with a night's fishing,' Dimitrios observed drily. 'Nothing like a night on the sea for clearing the mind.'

'I don't think that particular brand of perfume is quite me,' Ria parried quickly, wrinkling her nose and nodding to the dried blood and dirt coating his shirt.

'Touché.' His blue eyes were bright. 'You've been very patient with me. I'll remove my pungent presence from the immediate vicinity and let you enjoy your last cup of coffee in peace. Can you be ready in an hour?' He stood up, stretching.

The invitation caught her by surprise although she had been waiting on tenterhooks for him to repeat the offer he had made last night since her first sight of him that morning. Her big grey eyes looked up at him gravely, her face troubled.

'I promise to be good,' he said mockingly, the old cynicism grooving deep lines by his mouth. 'We will disappoint Christina if we don't go. She is of the opinion we are neglecting your Greek education.' He sounded bored by it all.

'Thank you, an hour will be fine,' she replied coolly, humiliation twisting her insides. It was plain he wasn't looking forward to a day in her company, and who could blame him? she thought wretchedly.

'Cheer up.' His voice was biting. 'Nikos will be home soon, I'm sure, and no doubt he will be quite happy to dance to whatever tune you want to play.'

'I don't want to play any sort of tune,' she said wearily, a small quiver shaking her voice.

'Are you sure about that?' His eyes gleamed hypnotically in the white light. 'Are you sure you don't want the relationship to pick up again now you have seen where he lives and your future possibilities?' he added insultingly.

She raised her head proudly, her eyes dark pools of anger. 'Quite sure.' Her voice was scathing. 'Whatever you may think of me, I can assure you I am no gold-digger. Nikos's wealth, or the lack of it, would make no difference to how I see the situation.' He couldn't doubt the ringing conviction in her tone.

'And how do you see the situation?' His face was shuttered but she felt something momentous was hanging on her reply.

There had been a subtle emphasis in his words she didn't understand.

'If Nikos was the last man on earth I wouldn't have him,' she said truthfully. 'I'm sorry,' she added as he winced at the harshness of the words, 'but you did ask.'

'That I did.' Suddenly, amazingly, there was a smile in the deep blue eyes as they looked at her just when she had expected one of his bursts of anger. She could feel her traitorous heart melting under his glance, and her look of astonishment at his next words was comical.

'I rather think I may owe you an apology.' She stared at him, her mouth half open.

'Christina pointed out a few home truths last night—she isn't too pleased with me at the moment.' He looked for all the world like a small schoolboy who had been reprimanded by his favourite teacher, and this new side to his complex personality was incredibly seductive.

'Oh?' It was all Ria could manage.

'I think I may have let past circumstances colour my judgement in certain areas,' he said stiffly. 'I had some time to think last night and I've come to the conclusion that you and Nikos must sort out your differences with no interference from anyone else. He isn't a boy any more and I'm sure there were faults on both sides.' He sounded a little as though he was trying to convince himself, a dark flush staining the bronzed face.

She suddenly knew she must tell him the truth, that if she lost this moment she would never find the courage again. 'Dimitrios—'

He interrupted her, his hand raised. 'However, I don't want Christina upset, so for a few days at least I shall expect you both to live under the same roof amicably. I'll have a word with Nikos and see what I can do.' A little muscle worked in his cheek. 'It won't be easy for him, you must appreciate that.' His eyes were warm on her flushed face. 'You are a very beautiful young woman.'

She stared at him, the words dying on her lips. She'd tell him later, she couldn't tell him now, couldn't bear to see that new softness in his eyes being replaced by the cynical coldness she was used to.

He left abruptly without another word, his big body straight and tall and his steps firm, having turned her world upside-down yet again. She was immersed in that strange feeling that only Dimitrios seemed able to create, that there were only the two of them on the whole planet and that everything paled into insignificance beside him.

Later, after spending a few minutes with Christina, who was looking surprisingly well and rested, and changing into lighter clothing, she hurried downstairs, her step buoyant and her heart singing at the thought of a whole day alone with him.

Dimitrios was sitting waiting for her as she entered the huge room, but as she neared him she saw he was asleep, his slow breathing steady and rhythmic. He was spread tiredly over one of the big grey sofas, tiny white lines of exhaustion pulling at his mouth and eyes. She crept stealthily to his side, unable to resist the opportunity to observe him while he slept.

The casual blue denim shirt and jeans he wore made him seem younger than his normal formal suit, and in repose his face lost its habitual watchfulness, the cold arrogance mellowing into relaxed mildness. He'd look like that first thing in the morning, she thought with a little pull at her heartstrings.

Almost without being aware of it, drawn by an irresistible longing, she brushed his mouth with her lips, her hand stroking back a wiry tendril of curly black hair from his forehead. As she did so he opened dazed blue eyes hazy with sleep and for a long moment they were both immobile, drowning in each other's gaze. Then with a tortured, muffled groan he pulled her soft body into his arms so that she was lying across his hard chest, her racing pulse echoing the beat of his heart. The kiss was achingly sweet, his firm lips gently exploring her quivering mouth until tiny tremors of excitement were shivering over her body in mounting desire, all her reason gone.

'You taste like honey,' he muttered unsteadily, his increasingly urgent caresses matching the growing hunger firing her body. His arousal brought a fierce primitive response in her lower stomach, a wild hot satisfaction that he couldn't hide his need of her.

'Heaven help me, what am I doing?' He sat up suddenly, thrusting her away with his abruptness and she sat silently back on her heels, trembling uncontrollably. 'You little Jezebel.' His voice was tender and he pulled her to him again at the sight of her white face, his touch gentle. 'Don't look like that.'

'Dimitrios?' she murmured against his chest, her voice muffled.

He moved to the edge of the sofa, putting her aside carefully, his face setting into its usual stern unapproachable lines. 'It's time we were going,' he said thickly. 'Go and see if Rosa has got the picnic hamper ready.'

'What did I do wrong?' Her voice was a tiny whisper.

He dropped his dark head forward, running shaking fingers distractedly through his crisp hair. 'You didn't do anything wrong,' he said slowly, bitter self-mockery evident in every word. 'You did it all too damn right.'

He turned suddenly, his eyes holding hers tightly. 'Let's just put everything on hold at the moment. You've got to see Nikos soon; let's just take everything from there.'

'Everything?' She gazed up into his grim face from her position at his feet, oblivious of the fact that her whole heart was burning in her eyes, her feelings for him written plainly on her glowing face.

He looked at her searchingly, faint hope warring with tenacious mistrust, and gave a little groan in the back of his throat. 'When you look at me like that with those great eyes promising the moon, you could make me believe black was white.' He shook his head gently. 'Why didn't you just hang on to Nikos and keep it all simple? I don't need this.'

He stood up sharply, the shutter coming down firmly over his face. 'Go and hurry Rosa up, there's a good girl.'

'But—' Ria began.

He lifted her up from the floor, his expression inscrutable. 'Go!' Ria went.

When he joined her a few moments later in the immaculate sunny kitchen it was as though nothing had transpired between them. He thanked Rosa gravely for the hamper—she fluttered distractedly in all directions, nearly dropping the dish she was carrying and turning as red as a beetroot. Lifting the large basket on to his shoulder, he called Ria to follow him out of the side-door which led on to the large paved area at the side of the villa. A whitewashed row of gleaming garages stood directly opposite housing various cars. Ria recognised the white Ferrari from the airport, and caught sight of a large blue Mercedes and two smaller sports cars in vivid shades of red and yellow.

'Are all these cars yours?' she asked in amazement as Dimitrios led the way to a large green Land Rover parked nearby. 'Not all,' he said briefly with a swift darting glance at her wide-eyed face. 'Christina uses the Mercedes and the yellow MG is Nikos's pride and joy. I can't believe he didn't extol the virtues of his Betsy!'

'Not that I remember,' she replied carefully, keeping her face expressionless with a great effort.

'Amazing.' He narrowed his eyes thoughtfully. 'Maybe you didn't have time to discuss cars.' The words were faintly insulting and Ria glanced at him warily. He was building walls again.

He helped her up into the high seat, which was covered with thick white towelling. 'The interior gets red hot during the day,' he explained quietly. 'By midday you will need the protection of the covers.'

She soon appreciated why the Land Rover had been chosen for the day's excursion. It was the perfect vehicle for the rocky winding coastline along which they were travelling. Ever the chameleon, Dimitrios became the perfect urbane companion intent on showing her the many changing faces of his homeland. They wandered slowly round ancient temple ruins, Ria dreamily trying to visualise the life of a long-dead civilisation until Dimitrios became impatient and called her back to the land of the living.

He showed her small quaint churches, beautifully cared-for and festooned with fresh flowers, windmills with canvas sails furled to tiny triangles, precipitously steep lanes and narrow alleyways where old grey-haired women swathed in black sat on their scrubbed steps selling hand-made basketwork and beautifully knitted shawls and tops.

At midday they parked the Land Rover in one old town and wandered along a warren of narrow streets, feasting at a local taverna on delicious canea cheese and fresh garlic bread washed down with a dry red wine. 'Kokkino,' Dimitrios informed her, making her repeat it again and again until she got the pronunciation right, laughing with her at the stumbling efforts to speak his tongue. She longed to reach out and take his hand, to make some overture to the world to proclaim them as a couple, but shyness coupled with uncertainty as to his response held her back.

Late in the afternoon, hot and tired, Dimitrios drove to a deserted beach and led the way to a tiny secluded bay unseen from the road. 'I wanted to show you this place,' he said laconically. 'It's a particular favourite of mine.'

She turned a glowing face to him to find him watching her reaction carefully. 'It's lovely,' she enthused warmly. 'I can't imagine there are many places on earth to equal this.'

'I've only ever brought one other person here,' he said blandly over his shoulder as he left to get the provisions from the Land Rover. 'Few people know of its existence so we shouldn't be troubled.' Her newly sensitised heart immediately leapt in anguish as she pictured a young Dimitrios alone with his first love in this idyllic setting.

'Please don't let it have been her,' she whispered into the slight breeze stirring the silver strands of hair on her shoulders, 'I don't mind anyone but her.'

The bay was entered by a tiny break in

the cliff strata, and once inside they were totally enclosed by warm rock pummelled silky smooth by years of turbulent weather. Soft white sand and deep blue sea formed a desert island image and Ria could almost believe they were the only two people alive in the world.

'Ready to swim?' His deep voice brought her out of the reverie she had fallen into as she stood dreamily watching the distant horizon.

'Oh!' She gasped in quick disappointment. 'I didn't bring my costume.'

'Choose one of these if you insist on wearing one,' he said drily, throwing a handful of minuscule bikinis at her feet. 'I always keep a few in the car with the towels and rugs. Nikos has a habit of arriving with a crowd of people and it's better to be prepared.'

'Where's yours?' Ria asked naïvely, and as she caught the mocking gleam in his laughing eyes she knelt hurriedly on the hot sand, inspecting the small scraps of material as though her life depended on it. When she raised her head it was to see Dimitrios nonchalantly disrobing a few yards away by the water's edge. His denim shirt and trainers were already lying on the white sand, and as she stared mesmerised first his belt, then his jeans followed. As his pants came down, exposing all of his finely muscled body to her rapt gaze, he turned and waved casually, chuckling wickedly at her quickly lowered head. He's doing it on purpose, she thought crossly, her cheeks pink; he's just trying to shock me. He certainly succeeded! that annoying little voice she couldn't always control whispered quietly in her brain.

Turning her back on him, she chose the bikini with the most covering potential and, draping a huge beach towel round her shoulders, changed quickly under the protecting folds. The tiny scraps of black material barely covered her full high breasts and the cutaway pants hugged her slim thighs seductively. 'Oh, well,' she muttered despairingly, feeling quite naked as she dropped the towel slowly, 'it's the best of a bad bunch and at least he can't blame the lack of material on me.'

Dimitrios was already swimming strongly in the clear turquoise water as she walked self-consciously down the beach, wilting under his approving gaze. 'I can't remember anyone else looking quite so delicious in that,' he called teasingly, his light tone belying the heat in his eyes.

She plunged hastily into the cold water, intent on hiding in the deep blue-green depths, and gasped as the coolness lapped silky soft against her hot sticky body. She moved further into the sea, diving down under the waves and surfacing just by Dimitrios who grinned lazily. 'OK?' She nodded dazedly, struck by the whiteness of his teeth in the darkness of his face and the way the small crystal droplets of water gleamed on his wet brown skin.

She dropped under the surface again, swimming down into that other world populated by small coloured fish and waving exotic plants, the bright sun lighting up the surface of the sea above her like a host of small moving diamonds. As she came up for air Dimitrios was beside her again, his strong arms cutting effortlessly through the small waves. 'Quite the little mermaid.' She felt ridiculously pleased by his praise, giving him such a radiant smile that he narrowed his eyes against it.

'Careful now,' he drawled mockingly, 'a mere man can only stand so much and I've been under a severe strain all day.' Not quite understanding what he meant and not really caring, she dived under the water again, swimming and floating to her heart's content until her body felt deliciously exhausted.

I don't think I'll ever be as happy again as I am today, she thought drowsily, looking up into the brilliant blue sky as she floated lazily on her back. The thought sobered her for a moment as a little chill stole over her body, the future suddenly hostile and uncertain.

The first razor sharp stab of pain shooting through her right leg caught her completely unawares, and as she gasped in instinctive fear both arms shot up and she sank beneath the surface, swallowing a disgustingly bitter mouthful of salt water. Desperately she struck out to the surface, managing one piercing scream before the excruciating pain curling her body into a tight sinking ball pulled her back down into the cold blue depths, sending blind panic coursing through her contorted limbs.

She searched for air and another mouthful of sea water flooded her mouth, burning her nostrils and filling her ears with the sound of death. She was drowning! In the few seconds before she felt her body going limp she called out blindly to her mother, willing her protection from above.

She didn't want to die, not now, not like this. As everything went black and the sound of roaring filled her ears she felt a force stronger than herself pulling her down, down, and the pain was still there, relentless and consumingly fierce.

CHAPTER FIVE

As Ria became conscious of the rock-hard arms pulling her up into the light she struggled dangerously in Dimitrios's firm hold, frantically pulling air into her bursting lungs, coughing and spluttering with the burning in her chest and twisting in agony as the pain knifed through her legs again, rendering her incoherent and blind with panic in his grasp.

He gently fought to hold her for a few seconds and then slapped her once very hard across the face. 'Relax, I've got you.' His voice was calm and controlled. 'Let your body go limp and I'll take your weight or you'll drown us both.' She sobbed with fear, clinging tightly to his neck, but as he continued to tread water slowly and talk patiently to her in that cool voice she lay back in his hold, still shuddering with pain and fright and coughing helplessly, but with the horror receding.

'Good girl,' he said soothingly, beginning to swim to the distant shore. 'You're quite safe and you're doing fine.' He kept up a reassuring slow monologue while his big powerful body cut through the water, carrying her effortlessly towards the haven of firm sand.

Once they reached shore he lifted her up into his arms, his anxious eyes sweeping her chalk-white face and bloodless lips, as again she winced with the clawing pain in her legs. 'Cramp?' he asked briefly, and as she nodded weakly he carried her quickly to where their sun-warmed rugs were lying, placing her carefully in the middle of them and pulling them round her body until she was cocooned in their heat. Kneeling down by her side he began to massage her legs vigorously and as the tightly bunched muscles began to relax Ria horrified herself by bursting into a torrent of tears, water gushing in an unflattering flood from her eyes, nose and mouth.

'It's all right, little one, cry it out.' Dimitrios gathered her into his arms, which shook slightly now the danger was over, holding her close to his damp chest and rocking her to and fro against his body as though she were a small child. He muttered low endearments into her tangled salty hair, slipping into his native tongue, his voice soft and tender. How long they sat like that Ria didn't know, but as her sobs subsided she began to feel slightly ashamed of her weakness and uncomfortably aware of the long hard naked body pressed so close to hers.

Her hot wet cheek was resting against his broad chest and the tiny dark curls of hair prickled against her soft skin tantalisingly, and as her arms loosed their grip from around the strong neck she was aware of a convulsive shiver that fleetingly shook the big frame. His hands moved the blankets around her body again, his touch jerky, and he rolled over on to his stomach a few feet away from her.

'Better now?' There was a tremor in the deep voice and she nodded shyly, having seen the evidence of his desire as he moved away, shaken and awed by the sight of his pure male beauty.

'I think I'd better have the equivalent of a cold shower,' he said drily, his face turned away from her, and with swift animal grace he rose and walked back down the beach, diving cleanly under the small foam-topped waves.

She lay back in the rugs, the ache in her legs slowly dying as the evening sun stroked her tired body with its warm fingers and with a little sigh she gave herself up to its ageless therapy, feeling too lethargic and bruised to move.

She was woken from a light sleep as Dimitrios flung himself down beside her, clothed again in his shirt and jeans, his brown feet bare. 'Come on, you shameless wench, get some clothes on,' he said lightly. 'I don't know about you but I'm starving.'

She struggled into her discarded skirt and top under the cumbersome towel again, wriggling out of the damp bikini with difficulty, vitally aware of Dimitrios's every move as he opened the hamper and poured two glasses of sparkling white wine.

'Drink that. You look as though you need it,' he said briefly as she moved to where he sat, making her suddenly aware of her tear-stained face and matted damp hair. Her hands moved nervously to the tangled mass and his face softened as he handed her the heavy crystal glass. 'I didn't mean it like that. You look just as beautiful as a poor little waif as you do normally.' His voice was unbelievably tender.

She looked at him solemnly, her grey

eyes enormous in her white face. 'I haven't thanked you for saving my life. I would have drowned out there if you hadn't have saved me.'

'Think nothing of it,' he said gently, running a big brown hand down her smooth arm. 'It's a hobby of mine rescuing damsels in distress. Just make me a promise you won't go swimming alone any time,' he continued, his expression hanging. 'What's happened once might happen again.'

She nodded obediently, swiftly drinking a glass of wine. She had a raging thirst.

'Hey, steady on.' He looked at the empty glass in surprise. 'If I'd have known you were going to swallow half the ocean I'd have brought some soft drinks too. I think you'd better eat. I can only just cope with you sober; tipsy...' He raised dark eyebrows reflectively.

Rosa had prepared a positive banquet and Ria discovered she was ravenously hungry. One large carton held fresh pink prawns nestling in a rich creamy sauce, another slices of various cold meats and tiny pasties and a crisp green salad. There were small crusty garlic rolls, two vegetable dips and several different cheeses, finishing with a selection of fresh sliced fruits for dessert. It was like no picnic Ria had ever experienced before. Everything had been kept deliciously cool in a large inner box and they ate hungrily in companionable silence until just empty dishes remained.

'That was out of this world,' Ria said gratefully, wiping the last of the prawn sauce from her mouth with a snowy white napkin and feeling much more herself again. 'Do you always eat like this?'

'Of course.' His expression was autocratic as though he suspected criticism. 'I work hard and play hard and I expect the best.'

'Well, you certainly get it,' she responded quietly, thinking he could be as prickly as a hedgehog.

'In some respects.' He leant over and refilled her wine glass, and she noticed he took great care not to come into contact with her body as he lay back on the rug, shutting his eyes against the golden pink glare of the dying sun. He had obviously regained perfect control of his emotions—why couldn't she feel the same? She looked at him stretched out like a big cat and apparently quite relaxed and remembered how his muscled body had looked as it gleamed in the sun. A little pulse beat at the base of her throat and she shook herself mentally, turning her attention to packing up the hamper and then walking down to the water's edge where daylight was rapidly fading.

'The land of the gods.' He made her jump as he came silently behind her, draping one of the small blankets round her shoulders. A small refreshing breeze had sprung up and the sea was bathed in a magical glow, the sky a myriad fiery rivers. A solitary bird swooped overhead, its harsh raucous cry jarring the peaceful rhythmic murmur of the waves. 'He's looking for his mate.'

She turned and found the steel-blue eyes fixed on her face. 'How do you know that?'

'I recognise a kindred spirit.' He stared at her for a long moment, his face intent as he searched her eyes. 'Ready to go?' he asked deeply, and she felt strangely disappointed as though something expected had not happened.

'I suppose so. It's been a wonderful day.'

He caught her arm as she went to move away, turning her in front of him roughly and looking down at her grimly from his great height. 'Why did you have to sleep with them?'

'What?' He had taken her completely by surprise and her grey eyes reflected her bewilderment.

'How many were there? Three, four?' The question was savage. 'Why couldn't you have waited? How can anyone look so fragile and innocent and behave as you do?'

She shrank from his rage, her face dark with fear. 'Please, Dimitrios...' Her voice was a whisper.

'Why do you do it?' His cold eyes seemed to probe into her mind and his voice was bitter and tormented as though a fierce internal battle was raging in that tall dark frame. 'How can I believe what your eyes and body tell me? You made Nikos feel as though he was the only man on earth. How do I know this isn't all some clever game? A trick to get off the hook.'

'You're hurting me.' His hand was biting into the soft flesh of her upper arm and she tried to pull away but he held her in an iron grip.

'I'd like to.' He shook her slightly. 'I'd like to open up that little head of yours and see what really goes on in your mind.

You are like two people in one body and both so different. One minute so pure and shy, the next...' The blue eyes flashed fire. 'How do I know which one is real?'

She lowered her head shakily, the thick fall of blonde hair hiding her white face from his hawk-like stare.

'You don't understand.' Her voice trembled and he shook her again, his fingers bruising her flesh.

'Make me understand, then. Tell me what's made you the person you are. Explain how you can make a man forget he won't be the first and maybe not the last. Talk to me, convince me.' The last words were a dark plea.

'Not here, not like this.' For the life of her she couldn't face telling him alone like this. She needed to ask for Christina's help, needed her alliance to deflect the white-hot rage this fiery Greek would feel when he knew he had been tricked again by a little English girl with silver hair.

He drew his breath in on a harsh deep sigh, his breathing laboured, and released his grip on her arm with a small shake of his head. 'I must be mad.' He was talking more to himself than her. 'To risk lightning striking twice...'

She sensed he was furiously angry with her, or himself, or both. He turned to her again, black head thrown back arrogantly, his hands thrust into his jeans pockets.

'I don't know whether to get you out of my system in the time-honoured fashion or see whether Nikos can throw some light on to the devious little puzzle you are.'

She stared it him, frightened to make any move that would release the devil that was holding him. 'You said back at the villa...'

'Yes?' he prompted, his voice resuming its usual cool sardonic note. 'What did I say at the villa?'

'You said you would wait till Nikos arrived. Before everything could be sorted.'

'I don't know if I want "everything" sorted,' he said sharply, red colour burning on his high cheekbones. 'For the first time in my life I don't know what I want, or maybe I do but it's too late for that. Three or four men too late. Oh, to hell with it.' He turned and strode back up the beach, leaving her hardly able to stand.

The ride back to the villa was conducted in almost total silence. Dimitrios drove fast and furiously, handling the large vehicle with masterly control, his face remorselessly cold. Ria sat huddled miserably in her seat, wishing she could turn the clock back to that first morning in her flat and start all over again.

Darkness had fallen swiftly, blanketing the landscape in a deep black veil, and as they neared the villa she could see that there seemed to be lights burning from every window.

'Not guests, not tonight,' Dimitrios muttered grimly as they pulled up in a screech of burning tyres outside the front of the villa, and as he cut the engine the heavy glass-panelled door was flung open and two figures, hand in hand, raced down the curving steps towards the Land Rover.

'Poppy!' Her startled exclamation was drowned in Dimitrios's call of welcome to his nephew. He gave her one swift glance of questioning concern and then the couple were upon them, their excited voices mingling with the frantic barking of the dogs. Ria caught a glimpse of Christina's stooped figure in the lighted doorway leaning heavily on her stick. She looked as though she had aged ten years since that morning.

The next hour forever remained seared

into Ria's memory. At first Nikos and Poppy had been oblivious to Dimitrios's stunned fury and their laughing voices offering involved explanations had seemingly gone on for ever until Ria could have screamed. Her whole being was aware of the still, tall figure standing to one side of the assembled throng, his splinter-sharp gaze never leaving her white face for a moment. She sat in dumb misery close to Christina on the sofa like a condemned prisoner awaiting execution until even Poppy's shrill voice faltered to a halt and a stillness of such magnitude crept over the room that even the dogs were silent.

'You cheating little liar!' When the storm broke it was of such savage ferocity that it brought everyone to their feet except its target. Dimitrios looked like a fiend from hell itself, his gleaming eyes so dark with burning rage that they seemed to glow red in the light from the lamps, his square jaw streaked with tight white lines that cut deep into his flesh. He had moved silently across the room to stand towering over her bent form, his hands clenched into tight hard fists in his anger.

'How dare you deceive me?' he snarled,

his voice dragged up from the depths of his body. 'All the time, from the first moment, deceit and lies!'

'I'm sorry,' Ria whispered in frozen terror, not daring to raise her head, aware of Christina moving her thin body between them as a buffer.

'Such treachery and you are sorry!' The words were like pistol shots, the first of a flood of vitriolic accusations that rained down on her fair head without end. He had lapsed into his native Greek but no one present could mistake his intent or his bitter anger.

'I have never before asked one of my guests to leave but I am telling you now, you leave as soon as there is a flight.' The last sentence was coldly final, all emotion burnt out.

Ria raised her streaming eyes to his at last, and the icy hatred she read there froze her blood. Why hadn't she told him before? Why was she such a coward? Finding out like this in front of everyone else had doubled the shock. Nothing could have been worse than this.

He gave her a last look of total contempt before turning to where Nikos stood with his arm protectively round Poppy, their young faces pale and horrified. 'The pair of you in my study at nine o'clock tomorrow morning,' he ground out through clenched teeth. 'You've got some talking to do and it had better be good.'

As he left the room, his face grey and as rigid as granite, Christina gave a heart-torn cry and stumbled after him, her face awash with tears.

Alone in her room Ria sat on the bed in frozen misery, staring at her white reflection in the mirror. This pain equalled the torment felt all those years ago when a tender-eyed young policewoman had told her that her whole family had been wiped out in one crazy blow. She could remember she had questioned and questioned the young woman until she had admitted they were all dead, killed by a drunk driver on his way home after a lunchtime binge. She had vowed then that she would never love anyone else so much again, never give anyone else the chance to hurt her as she was hurting now. And she had succeeded in her solitary life until a big dark stranger had rudely broken down all the fences she had built so carefully.

'I hate him,' she told the wide-eyed ghost in the mirror, 'I really hate him.'

But it was futile to lie to herself; she loved him with all her heart and how she was going to face taking up her normal life once again without breaking into a million pieces she didn't know.

She shivered in the warm night, covering her haunted face with hands that trembled. She couldn't bear to look at her strange image any longer. Wave after wave of pointless recriminations swept her mind until at last, exhausted and empty, she lay down on the bed, curled into a small tight ball, feeling like a little wild animal that had been hunted to the end of its strength.

'Ria, Ria, open the door.' She awoke to Poppy's persistent voice calling her name and was amazed to find it was morning. A long shudder racked her tired body as the cataclysmic conclusion to the previous day flooded over her in a black deluge, and she padded wearily to the door, surprised to find she must have locked it in her agony of mind the night before.

Poppy was waiting outside holding a tray on which a steaming pot of coffee and some hot buttered toast reposed. 'You look ghastly,' her cousin stated cheerfully as she marched into the room, setting the tray down determinedly. Ria's heart sank as she noticed two coffee-cups. This was obviously going to be a heart-to-heart and she didn't feel strong enough to fend off any searching questions Poppy would be sure to raise. Tact and diplomacy had never been high on her cousin's list of accomplishments.

'What on earth's been going on?' Poppy began, true to form. 'Nikos has never seen his uncle so mad. Usually he's Mr Cool but you seem to have got under his skin good and proper.'

'Save it, Poppy.' The flippant tone was grating on Ria's raw nerves. Surely even her thick-skinned cousin could see there was more at stake here than a casual misunderstanding?

Poppy studied her white face thoughtfully, the teasing light dying from her brown eyes. 'Oh, no, Ria, you haven't fallen for him, have you?' she asked in genuine concern. 'Not you, not the original ice-maiden.'

'I said leave it.'

Poppy wouldn't be told. 'You've certainly picked a winner to cut your puppy teeth on; he eats women for breakfast!

Nikos said they flock round him in droves, he's always—'

'One more word and so help me, Poppy, I'll hit you!' She meant it, and as Poppy looked into her burning face she realised it was a new Ria who was gazing at her with such dislike. 'Why do you always think you can barge in just saying what you like to who you like?' Ria was furious. 'When will you begin to realise that what you say and do can hurt people? Badly? I'm in this mess because of you so just leave me alone if all you can offer is gossip and mockery.'

'I didn't—' Poppy began, but Ria hadn't finished.

'Over the last few days I've been asked about things I didn't have a clue about and accused of things I don't like to think about. Dimitrios has questioned my morals from the first moment he met me and with your help I've confirmed every low opinion he has of the opposite sex.'

'I didn't ask you to pretend you were me,' Poppy said sulkily, flicking back her red hair pertly.

'Don't worry. From now on you're on your own,' Ria said grimly, her eyes shadowed. She had forgotten how totally

142

self-centred her beautiful cousin was.

'Please, Ria, don't quarrel with me,' Poppy began with one of her swift changes of mood. 'I'm truly sorry for all the trouble I've caused, and I do love you, really. I know you did it all for me and I am grateful, honest.'

Ria looked at her wearily, unable to resist the appeal in those big brown eyes. Poppy and her father were all the family she had and she owed them both so much.

Seeing her weaken, Poppy caught her hand, pulling her over to the small balcony, her flame-coloured curls catching the sun's rays and turning her small head into a blazing halo. 'Come and sit down and I'll explain everything while we eat,' she cajoled prettily. 'I'm going to need something to sustain me before I see Dimitrios this morning.'

Ria took a deep breath of the clear morning air. It was still very early and a golden haze hung over the garden, softening the outlines beyond. The air was rich with the smell of fresh warm bread drifting up from the kitchen where Rosa was busy preparing breakfast, and the aroma of newly percolated coffee teased her nostrils. Suddenly life seemed more hopeful. What she had done she had done to protect Poppy. When he had had time to think about it surely Dimitrios would understand that, and if he wasn't able to forgive her maybe he would at least appreciate her motives? Her back straightened and her small chin jutted out. It was done now, anyway. All the balls were in his court. She didn't have to lie or pretend any more.

'How long have you known Nikos?' she asked her cousin as they seated themselves on the balcony, pulling her towelling robe more tightly around her. The morning was still young enough to give a little nip to the air.

'Oh, ages,' Poppy replied airily, and as Ria raised her eyebrows she laughed a little shamefacedly. 'Well, four months is ages to me. You know what I'm like.'

'And how,' Ria replied with great feeling, her face straight. She wasn't ready to capitulate totally yet.

'He was over on business for Dimitrios,' Poppy continued, munching her way through a slice of toast as she talked. For once Ria's appetite had left her completely but she sipped the hot sweet coffee gratefully. 'I thought he was different from the start. Honest, I did,' she added, seeing Ria's look of disbelief.

'Well, if you thought that what has all the fuss been about?' Ria asked bewilderedly. 'Are you back with him now or what?'

For the first time that she could remember Poppy couldn't meet her gaze. With one of her swift graceful movements, carefully nurtured for her work but now second nature to her, her cousin rose and moved over to the edge of the balcony, leaning over and staring at the garden below, her slim back suggesting defiance. 'You aren't going to like this,' she said warningly, her voice mutinous. Ria's heart sank—what now?

'I'm expecting Nikos's baby.' Whatever she had expected it wasn't that, and at her horrified exclamation Poppy swung round like a small tigress, the quick temper that walked with her red hair clearly in evidence.

'Oh, don't go getting on your high horse! We'll have enough to contend with when we tell the lord and master this morning!' Ria sat for a moment trying to absorb what Poppy had told her, her mind racing. She felt deeply shocked but even as she did so she realised that all she had learnt over the past few days about the secret side of her cousin's life should have prepared her, at least in part, for this revelation.

'We didn't mean it to happen.' Poppy's voice was miserable. 'I've been around a bit and I should have been more careful. Nikos is such an innocent.'

'Was,' said Ria drily.

'But *he* is different,' Poppy continued earnestly. 'With him I didn't stop to count the cost. He could make me feel, oh...I can't explain, just fantastic.' A slight flush rose in Ria's cheeks. How could she in all honesty condemn her cousin when Dimitrios's slightest touch could make her forget the rest of the world existed? And if he had loved her, as Nikos did Poppy, could she have applied a brake?

She caught her breath on a sigh of mixed pain and longing. 'Why did you disappear?'

Poppy slumped against the warm stone despondently. 'I know—it was stupid, wasn't it? But when I found out I was pregnant I think I must have gone crazy for a week or two. I suddenly couldn't take all that commitment. I felt Nikos had rushed me to get engaged but I suppose in

146

the back of my mind I thought I could get out of that if I wanted to. But a baby!' Her voice trembled. 'I had to get away and sort out my mind before I told anyone, even Nikos.'

'You mean you didn't tell him about the baby?' Ria asked, appalled.

'No,' admitted Poppy slowly. 'I just told him it was over and bolted. One of the girls at the agency put me up for a few days and I began to think things through. Once I'd made the decision to keep the baby I knew I had to tell Nikos, so I phoned him here and he came straight back to England. Her face lit up. 'He was so thrilled, I couldn't believe it. I do love him, Ria.'

'Do you?' Ria's voice was sharp. 'Are you really sure about this, Poppy? You can't keep playing with people's lives as you've done all your life. There won't be just you and Nikos to consider in a few months but a very small person who will be totally dependent on you for everything. If you don't love Nikos enough to make a lifelong commitment, no amount of money will compensate for bringing a child into an unhappy home. It would be better adopted or with just you. You must be sure.'

'I am sure,' Poppy said sulkily, her face red.

'Well, if you are then both you and Nikos will have to work at your relationship. It won't be all wine and roses, you know. You are going to find this culture very different from ours and he won't be used to the English way of doing things. You'll both need to adjust.'

'How very wise.' The deep voice was icy cold and as both girls swung round Dimitrios stepped calmly through the open doorway, his dark face implacable. The small balcony immediately felt crowded as he settled his large frame into one of the small chairs, crossing his long legs and leaning back in his usual position with his hands clasped behind his head. His white shirt was open at the throat, his black hair slicked back from his forehead damp from an early morning shower, and he was the epitome of cold menace.

'I gather you are encouraging your cousin to stay here?' His narrowed gaze swept over them both and Ria felt her racing heart leap into her throat. He was so distant and cruel, so different from the companion of yesterday.

'Not at all.' She faced him squarely,

148

unaware that with her tumbled fair hair falling in a silver cascade around her slim shoulders and her pale face free of make-up she presented an ethereal picture in the soft morning light.

'It sounded like that to me.' His steel-blue eyes raked her face sharply.

'Well, if you listen to other people's conversations you must expect to get less than the full story.' She heard herself defy him with mounting horror and out of the corner of her eye she could see Poppy's rapt fascination with the proceedings change to unconcealed apprehension.

'Really?' he snapped viciously, levering his powerful body out of the chair, his predatory eyes never leaving her white face. 'I think it's a little ironic for you to presume to give me a lesson on morals.'

He swung round to Poppy, making her jump. 'Downstairs, now!' he ordered, his face arrogant. 'Nikos is already waiting in my study—join him there.' She left without so much as a glance at Ria, scuttling out of their presence with an air which looked suspiciously like one of relief.

'Now as for you,' he continued, his voice becoming dangerously soft, 'you will wait here until I return. This time, my little will-o'-the-wisp, we are going to have a question and answer session that the gods themselves wouldn't dare interrupt.'

She stared at him dumbly, drinking in the sight of him in spite of herself. There was a subtle seductiveness in his mastery that she was unable to fight even if she had wanted to. She had wondered in those bleak chilled hours before she had fallen into an exhausted sleep if he would pack her off back to England without seeing her again, and the thought had filled her with overwhelming despair.

He turned to leave, pausing momentarily as he brushed past her to touch the violet shadows under her eyes with a caressing finger. '"What a tangled web we weave, when first we practise to deceive."' His voice was mocking and cold but his touch was curiously gentle, the sky-blue eyes unfathomable.

After washing her hair and soaking the strain of the night away in a warm perfumed bath, she dressed quickly in a white sundress, applying a light touch of mascara to her thick lashes and letting her damp hair hang over her shoulders to dry. The sun was a white-hot ball now, the gentle heat of morning dispelled by its glare.

She sat waiting for him on the balcony, wishing she could go and find Christina and explain her actions to her, but not daring to risk Dimitrios finding her gone. The fragrance of flowers was heavy in the still air, drifting up from the slumbrous garden below. Pots of geraniums stood close to the wall along one side of the floor, their scarlet flowers brilliant in the clear light. A tiny multicoloured beetle was idly making its way along one terracotta pot, seemingly intent on its laborious journey until it suddenly opened transparent wings and flew into the sunlight. 'You're lucky,' she told the departing insect enviously, 'you can just fly away.'

She sensed Dimitrios's arrival a few moments later as he moved silently on to the balcony; he was as light-footed as a wild jungle cat. He stood in the doorway, his face closed.

'Why do you live alone in that flat?' The unexpected question caught her unawares and she stared stupidly at him, unable to collect her thoughts. She had anticipated more harsh recriminations or cynical mockery and the quiet conversational

151

tone of his voice rendered her speechless.

'You look at me as though you are scared to death.' The voice was still easy but with that warning edge that spoke of mounting emotion. 'Well, you haven't answered my question.'

'I suppose I just wanted somewhere that was totally mine,' Ria replied at last, nervousness making her voice quiver slightly. 'My parents had left the money in trust so there were no financial difficulties and my uncle thought it was a good investment.'

'Poppy explained the circumstances,' he said quietly. 'I'm sorry I jumped to the wrong conclusion about the flat originally but you must see how it looked to me. I understand it is just a normal working relationship with your boss?'

He was still watching her closely, his sharp eyes sweeping every contour of her face. 'We get on well but that's all,' she replied shortly, her voice cool.

'He is a friend?' The dark voice was quizzical.

'He's my employer and we work closely together.' She stared at him defiantly. 'He's been very fair to me.'

'Good for Julian,' he said blandly, 'but

I wouldn't say he has done you any favours. Working all hours, no social life—do you mean to say you actually enjoy that existence?'

'I gather that's Poppy's interpretation you're quoting?' Ria asked scathingly, really angry for the first time that morning. 'Just because I don't happen to enjoy stripping down to next to nothing for my living, it doesn't mean I'm some sort of freak, you know. I do enjoy my job, as it happens. It might not be glamorous and admittedly it wouldn't suit nine out of ten girls but I like it. I like the hard work, I get to travel and meet people; it's all I want at the moment.'

Or all I did want, she corrected silently in her mind as she stared at his cold face, his chiselled features mockingly dispassionate.

'Then you are a very lucky little girl, aren't you?' His rapier-thin voice sliced coolly into her anger. 'It's not many of us who are entirely satisfied with our lot.'

'Anyway, I thought it was Nikos and Poppy we needed to discuss,' Ria said quickly, afraid he might decipher her thoughts with that sharp computer brain.

'What gave you that idea?'

'Well, that's the important thing, isn't

it?' Her voice was suddenly weary. 'That's what this mess is all about.'

'Oh, I see. That's what it's all about.' There was a stillness to his face she didn't understand but it chilled her soul. 'What do you expect me to do? Congratulate them both and tell them how clever they have been?'

'Of course not!' Ria flashed back, stung by the scornful tone of his voice. 'They've been stupid, but I would have thought you of all people would understand how easy it is to make a mistake when you're young.'

As soon as the words left her lips she knew she had made a grave error. The brooding look on his face vanished and he swooped on her like a great hawk, catching her slim wrists in an iron grasp and pulling her roughly to her feet. 'Now who's been telling tales out of school?' he asked darkly, his eyes metallic with rage. 'You know nothing about it! How can an inexperienced little thing like you begin to understand about life and love? You live in some ivory tower where everything is black or white. The real world isn't like that!'

'Don't tell me about the real world!' He had hit her on the raw and her voice throbbed with violent emotion. 'I know enough about the real world to hate it! A world where a man can kill three people in one swoop and be let out of prison in three months. Three months!' Her voice caught in her throat. 'A month for a life!' Her voice was rising and she couldn't stop it, the things she had been silent about for so long spilling out into the open. 'But at least I can still believe in the good of people, which is more than you can! The world might be sick but people still rise above it when they get the chance. I could have given up lots of times and become bitter and twisted like you, but I didn't. I just chose to cope with my circumstances in my own way. It's not easy to forgive, I know that, but I also know that if you hold on to destructive thoughts you are the one who is destroyed. For every bad person there are a hundred good ones.'

She stopped, struck by the hard brilliant glow in his eyes as his gaze sharpened on her white face and stormy grey eyes. 'So you think you've got all the answers?' The words were cuttingly cruel.

'No,' she said wearily, realising the hard wall he had built round his heart was impenetrable. 'As I said, we all deal with our circumstances in our own way.'

'Then do me the courtesy of minding your own business,' he said coldly, 'and keep your theories to yourself. My thoughts are my own concern, but one I will share with you is that I'm not at all sure this new image suits you. How much you have concocted with that bit of candyfloss down there,' he nodded downstairs, 'I don't know, but don't think you will fool me again so easily.'

'Well, I won't be around to fool you or otherwise, will I?' Ria said hopelessly, turning and looking out towards the distant hills. 'As soon as I can I'll leave you all in peace.' If she had been looking at him she would have seen a shadow pass over his face and a slow tightening to the hard cruel mouth.

'Perhaps you might like something to remember me by?' he asked broodingly, turning her round before she could guess his intention and claiming her mouth in a burning, searing kiss. She struggled wildly, smelling the familiar tang of his aftershave with a tightening of her stomach muscles and knowing she was fighting herself as much as him.

'You can't resist me,' he murmured

against her cheek, relinquishing her mouth for a second. 'Whatever you think of me I can make you want me, can't I.' It was a statement not a question. She began to feel her body melt as the iron hand of his arms pressed her into his rigid body, the blood pounding in her ears.

'Don't! Leave me alone,' she gasped frantically, but, as his cool lips travelled slowly along her throat, gently kissing the rapid pulse and continuing upwards over her ears and closed eyelids, she knew with a feeling of panic that she was lost.

With a little moan she trembled slightly as he devoured her mouth again in a searching kiss, responding to his expert mastery of her body with instinctive desire. As she felt his passion mounting, a fierce excitement spread through her limbs, tiny tremors beginning to shake her legs as she clung on to his broad-muscled back for support. He probed the sweetness of her mouth greedily, moving her almost without her being aware of it into the privacy of the bedroom.

He bent her backwards so that she fell on to the softness of the bed, joining her a second later, his heavy-lidded eyes triumphant and fierce. Still covering her face with burning kisses, he let his hands have free rein over her gently shaking body, tuning her to his desire like an experienced musician with a violin.

As his hands and mouth worked their subtle magic she arched and twisted with little cries of amazement, unable to breathe as sensation after sensation washed over her body in a burning flood. He stopped for a brief second, surprised at her reaction, looking down at her dishevelled body with narrowed eyes that held a burning question in their depths.

'Do you still want to leave?' he whispered into the soft folds of her hair as his hands caressed her body knowingly. 'Do you think anyone else can make you feel like this?'

Ria shuddered convulsively, lost in a strange new void of desire where only his hands and mouth seemed real, moving her head brokenly from side to side as the ache inside her became a torment.

He claimed her mouth again in a kiss that was breath-takingly tender, fuelling the fire that was threatening to burn her up, and as he held her close to his long frame she groaned his name again and again into his warm lips.

He straightened slightly on to one elbow

and she whimpered as he moved away, looking up at him with blind eyes.

'Ria?' He whispered her name gently against her hot cheek. 'I need to know: would I really be the first?' She heard him through a thick mist of sensation, lost in whirling emotion. 'Answer me; would I?' His voice was persistent and she nodded dazedly, lost in her blinding love for him, unable to orientate her thinking.

'But how can I be sure?' The words were a tortured groan of self-loathing, and with a smothered oath he lifted himself from the ruffled bed, expelling a deep breath as he turned and walked out on to the balcony with catlike grace.

She lay immobile for a few seconds, unable to believe he had really left her, and then, as cold reason trickled icy despair over her body, she sat up hastily, adjusting her clothing with hands that trembled.

It had all been a coldblooded exercise! She remembered his whispered questioning with a stunned heart. He had been trying to see if Poppy had been telling the truth about her cloistered lifestyle and lack of male company. Why hadn't he obtained the ultimate proof? Her face burnt as she realised she would have been unable to stop him; she was putty in his hands.

Maybe she had proved to be too inexperienced to provide any real challenge, the ultimate easy conquest! Who knew what went on in that cold mind? She looked to where his dark shape was visible through the flimsy lace curtains and knew a moment of crushing humiliation so deep that she wished the ground could open up and swallow her. He had taken her unquestioning love and ground it under his heel. If he had wanted to punish her for her deceit he was succeeding beyond his wildest expectations. How could she have been so weak as to put the bullets in the gun he would surely fire at her?

CHAPTER SIX

It took all the courage Ria possessed to join Dimitrios on the balcony a few minutes later, convinced his face would be cold with a mixture of contempt and triumph, but as she stepped wearily through the curtains, head held high but two bright spots of colour burning on her cheekbones, she caught a fleeting glance of confused misery twisting the strong features before he swiftly turned his head.

'I'm sorry.' The deep voice was flat. 'That wasn't planned, you know.'

'I don't believe you.' Her voice was stark and brittle with pain. To think a few minutes ago she had been on the verge of succumbing completely to this harsh cruel man who patently despised her. She must be crazy! It frightened her that she couldn't recognise herself any more, because she knew even now if he was to touch her again history could repeat itself.

'What do you think?' His eyes were keen

as he turned to trap her in their hold. 'That it was some kind of twisted retribution for all your deceit?' It was so close to her thoughts that she blushed furiously, her face betraying her.

He made a gesture of impatience, his face stiff. 'I'm sorry that your opinion of me is so low, but strange as it may seem I came here today with the intention of trying to understand you better. I can see now it was a fruitless exercise.' His eyes were sharply critical. 'It seems I have no choice in accepting Poppy into my family and I thought if we could at least part on speaking terms it would prove...more comfortable for the future. That—' he flicked his head in the direction of the bedroom '—was an unfortunate mistake.'

Ria swallowed convulsively. A mistake, just a trivial mistake! In that moment she hated him. 'I can't look at it quite like that,' she said painfully.

'Good grief, girl, it was no big deal, was it? Nothing happened, I'm sure you must have indulged in the odd passionate clinch before.' Even as he spoke the words there was a waiting look about his face, a stillness in his eyes she couldn't fathom.

'No, I haven't, as it happens.' She forced

the words out through pale lips, and as the dark eyebrows raised consideringly she had the feeling he was playing with her, testing her out in some weird way that made sense to him.

'Do you mean to say you've reached the age of twenty-one—you are twenty-one, aren't you, or was that a lie too?' She nodded the answer. 'You've reached twenty-one,' he continued mockingly, 'and kept all those charms under wraps? I can't believe that.'

'I don't care what you believe,' she said stonily. 'I don't have to explain anything to you. You are nothing to me.' She wanted to hurt him, to see some spark of emotion in that tauntingly cool face, and as her words registered in his eyes she saw a small flame of anger ignite.

'I think it's best for both of us that you are leaving soon.' His face was as cold as flint. 'You have caused enough havoc in our lives. We don't need...' He stopped abruptly as the anguish in her soft grey eyes reached him, and swore softly and vehemently under his breath. 'Stop it!' He took her by her arms and shook her gently as a tiny muscle in his jaw contracted. 'Stop looking at me like that.' He flung her aside as though her flesh burnt him, disappearing through the doorway with that lithe panther-smooth walk peculiar to him.

Ria stood quite still, feeling as though she were shrinking down into a tiny atom of nothingness. I can't take any more of this, she thought wretchedly. He can pick me up and drop me down as though I'm a toy. I must get away.

That thought stayed with her the rest of the long morning. Nikos and Poppy had disappeared after the talk with Dimitrios and Christina had left instructions with Rosa that she wasn't to be disturbed. Dimitrios seemed to have vanished off the face of the earth, for which she was supremely grateful. She couldn't have faced him so soon after the traumas of the last twenty-four hours. After a solitary walk along the dusty cliff-top in the fierce heat she returned to the villa at midday and ate the light lunch Rosa had prepared in her room, before stretching out on the soft bed intending to rest her aching eyes. She must have fallen asleep, for she awoke with a start as a light tap sounded at the closed door, surprised to find evening shadows darkening the warm room.

'Come in.' She sat up blinking in the soft light to see Christina open the door quietly and moved hesitantly into the room, her expression apprehensive.

'I'm sorry to wake you, my dear.' Ria was relieved to find the older woman was still speaking to her and surprised to see her face so friendly. 'I've been asleep myself most of the day; yesterday took more out of me than I had thought.'

Ria rose swiftly from the bed and took Christina's cold hands in her own warm ones, her face earnest. 'Please believe that I never meant to hurt anyone,' she said urgently, feeling it was imperative to convince Christina of her motives. 'I was only trying to help Poppy and it just seemed the best thing to do at the time. I know it must seem incredibly stupid to you but I really thought I could make things easier for you.'

'Dimitrios has already explained his visit to England,' Christina said slowly, her voice registering disapproval. 'I feel he is the instigator, possibly for the highest motives, of this disastrous episode. I'm amazed at him. I suppose he swept in on you with all guns firing, so to speak?'

Ria nodded ruefully and Christina shook

her head in annoyance. 'There are times when I could almost think our father lives on,' she said quietly, her eyes sad. 'He isn't a hard man really, despite what you may think. There is still the original Dimitrios there somewhere, locked away deep inside. I know it.'

Ria looked at her hopelessly. 'Well, I haven't got the key to unlock the magic box,' she said, her eyes speaking volumes. 'I think he really hates me now.'

'Don't you believe it,' Christina said briskly, her eyes suddenly bright. 'Would you like to have the key?' The question was unexpected but Ria answered immediately from the heart, her eyes tight on Christina's lined face.

'More than anything,' she replied, 'more than anything. But you mustn't tell him.' She caught hold of Christina's arm in sudden panic. 'Please, Christina, promise me you won't tell him.'

'Oh, Ria.' Christina shook her head, on which white hairs were beginning to outnumber the black. 'What a tangle.'

'Promise me,' Ria persisted.

'I promise,' Christina said reluctantly, her face soft with pity. 'You are such a child, my dear. Your cousin is more than capable of taking care of herself; I'm amazed you are the same age.

'Anyway,' she changed the subject understandingly, her eyes gentle on Ria's flushed face, 'Dimitrios and I had a long talk this morning. I don't approve of what's happened but what is done is done. My son and your cousin need to get married as quickly as possible as far as I can see.' Ria stared at her blankly. She had expected Christina to be overwhelmed with shock and disgust, but here she was taking charge of the situation as though it was the sort of thing that happened to them every day.

'Can you stay here until Poppy is married?'

Ria stared at her in horror. She couldn't stay here, close to Dimitrios, seeing him every day. 'I c-can't,' she stuttered anxiously, her mind racing. 'I have to go home.'

'I don't want to pressurise you, but there are a lot of arrangements to make in a very short time.' Christina's voice was faintly pleading. 'It would be an enormous weight off my mind if I had someone reliable to help me.' Ria remembered with a jolt the reason Dimitrios had come to fetch Poppy originally. Christina was ill. Of course she couldn't cope all by herself, and Ria knew from experience that Poppy would be of little help.

'How long will you need me?' she asked slowly, and Christina smiled gratefully, her body relaxing.

'I think we can manage to get things completed within a month,' she replied hopefully. 'Maybe six weeks.' Ria nodded in resignation. It looked as though she was well and truly stuck here for the foreseeable future.

Dinner was an uncomfortable affair with Poppy red-eyed and silent and Nikos quietly grim. Dimitrios was his usual laconic self, his eyes lazy on the assembled throng, softening only when they rested on Christina's troubled face. Christina left them before coffee, pleading a headache, and after they had finished the meal Dimitrios beckoned to Ria imperiously as she made to rise from the table.

'I want a word with you.' His eyes moved slowly over her face, lingering for a second on the softly parted lips. 'Come into the garden for a moment.' She followed him obediently in a daze, leaving the other two sitting morosely at their coffee, feeling a tingle in her lips as though he had kissed her. Pull yourself together, she thought, irritated with her blatant weakness where he was concerned.

'This has been a bigger shock to Christina than she is admitting,' he began immediately they were seated in the velvet darkness, the soft perfume of the day still hanging in the air. 'I don't want her making herself ill with all the preparations. Would you be prepared to stay on for a while and assist her?'

Ria stared at him in surprise, her grey eyes huge in the dull light. 'Hasn't she told you?'

'Told me what?' he asked shortly, his face autocratic.

'She asked for my help this evening,' Ria said quietly. 'I told her I would stay as long as I am needed.' A small muscle twitched in his cheek at her words but otherwise his face was still.

'I'm grateful.' He didn't sound it. 'As far as I can see Poppy will be of no help at all,' he continued bitingly, his lip curling slightly as he said her unfortunate cousin's name.

'What do you mean?' Ria countered carefully, agreeing privately with his opinion but not daring to show it.

'Let's just say, a lot of things have fallen into place since last night,' he replied coldly. 'It all makes sense now.' Ria looked at him uncertainly, unsure of his meaning, noting the piercing steel in his glance. She knew him well enough now to recognise that look and understood Poppy's discomfort during dinner.

'Poppy's all right,' she defended weakly. 'A bit thoughtless at times but her heart's in the right place really...'

'Oh, she does have one, then?' he asked crisply. 'When do we get to catch a sight of this phenomenon?' As she went to reply he motioned her voice away, moving closer to her so her treacherous heart lurched alarmingly. 'There is such a thing as being too loyal, you know,' he said quietly, his eyes sweeping her face. 'I would have thought you had learnt that by now.' Ria gazed up mesmerised into the dark face above her, unable to reply.

'You'll take care of Christina for me?' This time there was no commanding authority in the deep voice but a concerned plea and she responded immediately, nodding her blonde head vigorously and fighting a terrifying impulse to reach up and touch that dark tanned cheek where black stubble was beginning to break through.

He stroked the top of her head thoughtfully, letting his hand slip down the silky softness to the nape of her neck and catching hold of the thin silver to let it slip slowly through his fingers. She shivered in spite of herself, his touch sending tiny darts of fire down her spine.

'You're very sweet.' His voice was thick and it did crazy things to her insides that she despised herself for but was unable to control. He drew away suddenly, letting his hands fall to his sides as he spoke. 'You'll be spared my presence for a week anyway.'

'What?' She wasn't sure if she had heard him correctly.

'I have to go abroad on business,' he explained briefly. 'I'm afraid I've let domestic difficulties take over for the last couple of weeks and I can't put this off any longer now.'

He turned back to her, his dark face cynical. 'Will you miss me?' His voice was sarcastic but with a tiny question mark that Ria's heightened senses caught.

'Yes,' she said simply, lowering her eyes as she spoke, frightened she would give too much away.

His eyes narrowed over her lowered face. 'We've got some things to sort out, you and I,' he said lazily, a tiny glow in the dark blue eyes. 'It will have to wait until I return but for now this will do.' He bent his head as she had been unconsciously hoping he would do for the last ten minutes, kissing her lingeringly, his lips firm and warm. The kiss was piercingly gentle, his mouth holding hers captive in sweet tenderness that was unlike anything she had felt before. There was no fierce passion in the kiss, just a breathtaking promise that seemed to touch her very soul. She swayed slightly as his lips left hers and she noticed that his hands were bunched tightly in his pockets as though to keep them immobile.

'I don't want you to be frightened of me,' he said slowly, his voice so low that her ears strained to catch the words, and as she caught her soft underlip in pearly white teeth he shook his black head thoughtfully, self-mockery twisting his features. 'Innocence is a terrible weapon,' he said puzzlingly, and as her eyes widened in bewilderment he touched her face with a hand that trembled slightly, turning and walking away through the darkness and whistling for the dogs, who appeared as though by magic.

I'll never understand this complex man, she thought hopelessly. One moment he seemed to hate her and the next... 'It's just animal desire,' she whispered into the quiet night, firmly quelling the treacherous hope that sprang unbidden into her mind. He would be a man of vast sexual appetite used to having his physical needs met by any woman he wanted. If what Poppy had intimated was true she could expect nothing more than to be counted as a handy diversion, holding limited attraction for him because of her likeness to his first lost love. 'Get that into your thick head, stupid,' she whispered to herself, fighting back the hot tears that pricked into the back of her eyes. 'You would just be the latest in a long line of affairs.'

As she walked into the dining-room the next morning feeling heavy-eyed and tired, Poppy's bright voice met her in a burst of greeting, high with excitement. 'Hi, Ria! Come on, sleepyhead, we've nearly finished! Come and have breakfast. This sea air makes me famished.'

Ria glanced over to where Nikos was

smiling indulgently at her cousin, their arms linked. Her whole manner was transformed from that of the subdued, crestfallen girl of yesterday. The reason for her buoyancy soon became apparent as she continued gaily, 'Dimitrios is going to take us to see a house in a minute. It's not far; you can come if you like.'

Ria looked at her in disbelief. 'A house?'

'Yes, you idiot, you know, four walls and a roof for the use thereof.'

'Are you sure you can afford a house?' Ria asked warningly. 'Maybe a flat or—'

'It's a wedding present!' They all jumped as the familiar deep voice growled through the open doorway from the shaded lounge. Ria caught Nikos's eye and he shrugged wryly.

'His bark is worse than his bite,' he said softly, but not soft enough.

'The bite can be quite nasty, believe me.' Dirnitrios appeared unsmilingly in the doorway looking unbelievably handsome in a light grey suit and snowy white shirt, his brown skin freshly shaved.

'Are you coming, then, Ria?' Poppy asked, rising from her chair, and Ria shook her head in quick refusal, feeling ridiculously unwanted. They had obviously

174

been going to go without her.

'Of course she is coming. Who do you think I've been waiting for?' Dimitrios's harsh voice was clearly directed as a rebuff and for once even Poppy's skin wasn't thick enough. She flushed and sank back down in her seat as he continued, 'After she has eaten, of course.'

It was half an hour's drive along dusty roads to reach the small cottage Dimitrios wanted them to see. Perched up high beside Dimitrios in the Land Rover, Ria tried to concentrate on the dazzling scenery which never ceased to stir her senses, every nerve in her body vitally aware of that big powerful body relaxed and silent beside her. Nikos and Poppy were cuddled together in the back seat, overt giggles and little sighs punctuating the air now and again. She caught Dimitrios's eye at one point and he smiled wryly. 'Shall I ask Nikos to drive?' She blushed furiously and was disconcerted to hear that deep chuckle rumble into the air. Every time! Why did she have to respond every time?

They passed clusters of white cuboid houses perched in untidy harmony on green-brown hills, the scorching sun already turning the young grass yellow. Every now

175

and again there was a glimpse of the sparkling turquoise sea, tranquil and still, and white beaches unmarred by any ugly high-rise hotels. She drank in the warmth and colour, sighing blissfully and stretching like a small satisfied kitten. Dimitrios glanced sideways, his face softening into an understanding smile. 'Makes you glad to be alive,' he said slowly, his eyes warm.

The cottage was situated on the outskirts of a small thriving town, standing by itself in a small enclosed garden. As they stepped through huge arched wooden doors into an enchanting tiny courtyard Ria caught her breath in delight. The floor of the courtyard was a mosaic of intricately hand-laid pebbles in traditional Greek design, and half of it had a roof of vine and bougainvillaea and a free-form sculpture of gnarled prickly pear. A riot of bright sweet-smelling flowers clung to the old stone wall, perfuming the air with a heavy richness.

As Dimitrios unlocked the old wooden door with a key he produced from his pocket, two tiny birds fluttered down on to the window-box, their small eyes brightly interested. 'Love-birds,' Dimitrios commented briefly in answer to her questioning gaze, his lazy glance following Nikos and Poppy into the cottage, wickedly mocking. 'Appropriate, eh?'

'I never know when you're serious or not,' Ria said as they followed the others into the small house, and he stopped her in the doorway, his touch gentle.

'It'd be fun teaching you,' he said suggestively, watching with satisfaction the hot colour sweep over her cheeks in a red tide. 'I'm just beginning to believe that is for real,' he whispered softly, running the tip of a forefinger across her smooth cheek, following the line into the hollow of her throat where a small pulse beat nervously at his touch.

'Please don't.' She was finding his tenderness so much harder to take than his cruelty. It was making her poignantly aware of something lost before it was even found.

His face tightened and he drew back immediately. 'Nice little place, isn't it?' he said mockingly. 'Somewhere where they can fight in peace.'

The cynicism hurt her as she suspected it was meant to. 'Doesn't anything reach you?' she asked wearily, wondering how anything could break through the ice round his heart. 'They'll maybe have the odd row but they'll be happy most of the time. Don't you want to get married one day and have children? Share things?'

Something flickered in the dark blue depths of his eyes and was gone, and with a twist of his body he moved her in front of his big frame through the doorway. 'Go and join the others.' His voice was husky.

Poppy and Nikos were enthusing rapturously when she joined them, their young faces alight with pleasure. The whole cottage had recently been renovated and the décor was light and modern, boasting a small compact kitchen with every modern appliance. A small extension at the back of the cottage housed a bright cheerful bathroom, and steep narrow stairs led to two good-sized bedrooms decorated in pastel shades, one with a built-in bed raised on a traditional high platform. The rectangular lounge downstairs led on to a small garden filled with flowers and small shrubs in hand-painted pots. The whole effect was one of smart gaiety.

'Do you like it?' Dimitrios's eyes were on Poppy's face, and she turned impetuously towards him, her arms going out in a hug and then freezing in mid flow. Ria knew just how her cousin felt. She didn't think she would have the nerve to fling herself unasked into his arms either.

'It's lovely,' Poppy said weakly, and Nikos nodded affirmation.

'I'll go and settle the details, then.' With a curt nod he strode out of the door and down the dusty road to the first row of whitewashed houses in the distance, a tall lonely figure.

'You hurt his feelings.' Nikos's voice was unusually cool as he looked down at his fiancée.

'Don't be silly,' said Poppy defensively, looking to Ria for support. 'He doesn't have any feelings.'

'Poppy!' The word was a sharp bark and for a moment Nikos looked and sounded exactly like his uncle. Easy tears flooded Poppy's eyes but Nikos had moved to the doorway, looking into the distance where Dimitrios stood talking to a small bent old woman shrouded in black.

'You don't know anything about him,' he said slowly, his back to the two girls. Ria had the distinct feeling he was talking to her as much as to Poppy. 'He's like the oyster, a hard exterior but a soft inside housing a pearl.' Poppy sniggered disbelievingly.

'Come on, Nikki,' she said scornfully, her voice strident. 'You can't tell me he's got a soft spot after that interview yesterday. I've never been spoken to like that in my life.'

'Perhaps it was long overdue, then.' The words were out before Ria could stop them and she looked aghast at her cousin, who glared back at her, her brown eyes black slits and her mouth a tight white line.

Nikos turned round, his handsome face wrinkled with fervour. 'He's done so much for the village,' he said, talking directly to Ria now, his voice low and rapid. 'He built a pharmacy and pays for the resident doctor to come out three times a week from the hospital in Marphos. He's put bathrooms in all the cottages—'

'You don't have to convince me,' Ria said gently. 'I'm not his enemy.'

Nikos shook his head. 'No, listen, I want you to understand.' She heard Poppy snort in the background, and, after a withering glance at his fiancée, Nikos took her by the arm and led her outside into the courtyard where the fragrance of a thousand summer days drifted in the golden air. Through the open arched door they saw Dimitrios follow the tiny figure into the house, and Nikos pulled her down beside him on a small wooden bench at one side of the old wall.

'Do you know how we came to have so many dogs?' he asked suddenly, and Ria looked at him in surprise. What did the dogs have to do with her finding out about Dimitrios?

'The only other dogs you'll see around here are half-starved little mongrels sniffing round the fishing-boats,' Nikos continued slowly. 'Greek families rarely keep pets. A few years ago when I was still at school an eccentric old French woman retired out here with a houseful of cats and dogs. When she died her family came over and sold the house but no one bothered with the animals. They just ran wild, scavenging food where they could until one of the larger dogs got killed and my uncle got to hear about it. He went down to the town where they were rounded up what was left of them and brought the lot home.'

He wrinkled his aquiline nose in smiling distaste. 'Mother was furious but she got used to it in the end. The only time she objects now is when one of the cats leaves a present of the odd dead mouse on her bed.' Ria shivered involuntarily.

'She asked Dimitrios why he did it one day and do you know what he said?' The bright blue eyes, so like his uncle's, looked at her hypnotically.

'No.'

'He said nothing should be abandoned without hope.' Ria stared at him, her stomach turning over at the thought behind the words.

'You'll have her in tears in a minute.' The deep voice was clearly unamused and as they turned to the open doors where Dimitrios stood Ria noticed the smile playing round his mouth didn't reach those watchful eyes.

Nikos stared at his uncle uncertainly, recognising his mood, and Dimitrios's face relaxed a little as he saw his nephew's apprehension. 'Go on, go and tell your beloved I've set the ball in motion,' he said mockingly. 'All the details should be settled within the month as the woman who is caretaking the place informs me that the owners are desperate to complete as soon as possible.'

'Thanks, Dimitrios.' Nikos's voice was

subdued but his eyes were bright with pleasure as Dimitrios walked across and gave him a brief hug.

'Just work at being happy, boy,' he muttered into the black hair, giving him a little push towards the house as though ashamed to show his emotion. 'You'd better finish this inspection quickly,' he added as Nikos disappeared into the cool interior. 'I need you to drop me off at the plant shortly.'

He walked over to the seat Nikos had vacated, sitting down beside Ria on the warm wood with a tired sigh and shutting his eyes. Everything was very still. There was no sound from the house and only the low buzzing of busy insects in the foliage dotting the courtyard broke the silence with a monotonous drone. Ria risked a glance at him under her lashes. His eyes were still shut and in repose the handsome face looked weary, small white lines cutting into the skin round his mouth and eyes.

There was something of the lean bandit in him even in the immaculate suit and handmade shoes. She could imagine him sweeping into a village on a coal black stallion leading a band of buccaneers intent on pillage and rape...

'Do you approve?' The low dry voice cut into her thoughts so effectively that for a horrible moment she thought he had read her mind.

'Approve?' She was grateful those piercing eyes were still closed as pink flushed her cheeks.

'The house,' he said patiently, 'do you like it?'

'How could anyone not like it?' Her voice was warm. 'It's a lovely little place, Dimitrios. You're so kind to help them.' Since her conversation with Nikos she was increasingly aware of that hint of loneliness surrounding him, more so when he was relaxed like now.

'I'm not totally unfeeling, you know.' His voice was dry and the heavy-lidded eyes snapped open. 'My nephew's happiness is very important to me.'

'What about your happiness?' Ria dared to enquire, half expecting a rebuff. 'Do you ever consider that?'

'Perhaps more than I have any right to, especially recently.' The words seemed torn out of him and he moved restlessly, his muscled thigh fleetingly brushing Ria's hip, sending a tingling down her leg. He turned in the seat to face her, that strange look that she had caught once before burning in his eyes. 'You have no idea how bitterness can warp the soul, little one. You were more right than you knew yesterday. It can work away at the inner man until something is gone, lost, never to be replaced. Youth should be matched with youth.' Ria felt she was losing the thread of the conversation, missing something that was of vital importance. His voice held such a consuming sadness and she didn't know how to help him.

'I should have apologised to you yesterday for my behaviour on the night Nikos and Poppy showed up,' he said suddenly. 'I intended to when I came to see you and then...'

Ria flushed scarlet, remembering the sweeping desire she had felt and their intimate embraces. 'It's all right, you don't need to apologise,' she said quickly. 'I deserved all I got and I couldn't understand half of what you said anyway.'

He looked at her sharply, his eyes wide with surprise, and then laughed softly in delight. 'You mean all that expenditure of energy was wasted?' He was teasing her again but it didn't matter; his face looked happier and that was all that mattered. Oh, I do so love you, Ria thought, lowering her eyes and letting her hair cover her face. Maybe there was a chance? She could love enough for both of them.

'Don't change, Ria.' He kissed the top of her fair head as he rose, his voice husky. 'I'm only just beginning to believe you are for real, so don't change.' He walked over to the cottage door, calling Nikos as he went and glancing at the gold watch on his tanned wrist.

'Hell, Nikos, get a move on!' he called sharply, all tenderness gone. 'I should be there by now.'

Once they had all piled into the Land Rover Dimitrios kept his eyes on the road, driving swiftly with total concentration. Within ten minutes they reached the entrance to a massive factory complex with rows of buildings stretching endlessly into the distance, secure behind an eight-foot steel-meshed fence patrolled by security guards with guard dogs at their sides.

The sun shimmered blindingly on the gates as they swung open, and Dimitrios stopped the car in a swirl of dust, reaching under his seat for a black leather briefcase and jumping down from the vehicle in one fluid movement.

'It's all yours.' He smiled to Nikos in the back. 'I'll be back this time next week if all goes well.' He moved round the car and for a second Ria thought he was going to walk away without a word of farewell, until she realised he was moving round to her door.

'Get out a moment.' He reached in a bronzed hand and helped her down from the high seat, his face closed and unsmiling. She landed nervously in front of him, the top of her head just reaching his shoulders, and he moved her round to the back of the Land Rover out of sight of the guards.

'Yes?' She looked up at him wide-eyed, her silver hair drifting round her face in the faint hot breeze that was blowing.

'I shall be gone a week,' he repeated, his voice gruff. They looked at each other for a timeless moment before he bent down, putting the briefcase on the sandy dirt and drawing her into his arms in a close embrace. 'I've got no right to make love to you, no right at all,' he murmured as his lips brushed hers gently, the kiss deepening as he felt her mouth open in response to his. His arms held her firmly but gently pressed close to his body, the scent of him filling her nostrils in an intoxicating perfume until she felt totally enclosed by his strength, protected and safe.

She reached up to put her arms round his neck, standing on tiptoe as she did so, and he suddenly lifted her off the ground in an enfolding bear-hug, pressing her closer and closer into his taut frame until she could hardly breathe. 'I want to eat you,' he growled. 'Do you have any idea of what you do to me?' She heard the words with a deep thrill at the same time as a little voice of caution whispered, Steady, girl, steady. It was only two days ago he ordered you out of his life. I don't care, she answered the inner voice wildly, I don't care. I'll take anything he gives now and let the future take care of itself.

A discreet little cough reminded them they weren't alone and he set her down reluctantly, the gleam in his eyes reflected in her own.

'Look after Christina for me.' He bent down for the briefcase, dropping one last fleeting kiss on her upturned face as he walked away without turning round again.

As he walked through the gates he was immediately surrounded by a group of men who had appeared from the nearest building and she could hear him barking orders in military style, his voice crisp and precise, rising over the other voices like an eagle soaring over a flock of starlings. She smiled to herself as she stood watching until they all disappeared out of sight, her last glimpse of his black head towering over the other men's bringing a lump to her throat although she didn't know why.

The future was still uncertain, he had made no promises and probably never would, but she knew one thing now with crystal clarity. Until he told her again to go she would stay here in this foreign land close to the man she loved.

CHAPTER SEVEN

The next few days passed in a blur of activity. After two days of intensive work Ria forced Christina to stay in bed; the older woman's white face and trembling hands frightened her and reinforced the promise she had made to Dimitrios in her mind. 'You can issue instructions from here,' she said as she tucked Christina under the covers as though she were a child. 'We need someone to keep a clear mind and organise lists.'

With Christina safe upstairs she threw herself into the preparations wholesale, doing the work of three people. It helped to dull the ache Dimitrios's absence caused in her heart, and it was a relief to fall into bed late at night too exhausted to think.

On the third day Dimitrios phoned Christina in the early evening when Ria was sitting enjoying a glass of wine with her in a rare moment of relaxation, the late golden rays of sun lighting up the bedroom with a warm amber glow.

Brother and sister exchanged rapid conversation in their native tongue and just as the call was ending Ria heard Christina mention her name, her face straightening as she put down the receiver.

'What have I done now?' Ria asked half jokingly with a twinge of apprehension tightening her voice. Christina shrugged lightly, her face guarded, obviously disinclined to comment. 'Did you tell him I was with you?' Ria persisted, and as the older woman nodded slowly she felt a hot shaft of pain spear through her chest. So he couldn't spare a minute to talk to her. None of it really meant anything to him—out of sight, out of mind.

'He had someone with him, my dear,' Christina explained, upset by the hurt in Ria's soft grey eyes. 'It was a little difficult for him.' Ria nodded, trying to control her features. She didn't want to distress Christina.

'He's a very busy man,' she said lightly, amazed her voice sounded so normal, and Christina agreed thankfully, glad the awkward moment had passed.

Life resumed its hectic pattern and Ria determinedly put the incident out of her mind; there were enough problems without her dwelling on fresh ones. Nevertheless the moment sowed a little splinter of doubt in her previously adamant mind.

It was a week since Dimitrios had left and Poppy was proving troublesome. The early days of her pregnancy were making her feel unwell and she was snappy and irritable; tempers were getting frayed. Even Nikos was nearing the end of his patience and Ria had felt like screaming more than once.

They were all sitting on the veranda having a long cool drink before dinner, the dogs spread out round their feet in a disgruntled heap. They were waiting for their master to come home and Ria could sympathise with them; she felt her ears were turned down and her tail had lost its wag.

'Let's take the dogs down to the harbour for a walk,' Nikos suggested suddenly after three heavy sighs from Poppy in the space of half a minute. 'It'll do us all good.'

'You go,' Christina encouraged them. 'Dinner will be another hour yet.'

The night sky was already turning pewter-dark as they wandered along the shoreline, talking quietly and listening to the gentle swish of the sea. Ria could feel herself slowly unwinding. She felt so tense all the time lately—perhaps things would be different when Dimitrios returned. Nikos and Poppy were hand in hand and she envied them their easy familiarity, her thoughts winging again and again to that big dark stranger she was no nearer understanding.

A cool night breeze was blowing and the stars were beginning to glow like hundreds of tiny diamonds as they walked back towards the villa, entering the grounds by the garden gate, laughing at some quip Nikos had made.

The dogs suddenly pricked up their ears in one movement, breaking into rapturous barks and hurling themselves up the garden in a frenzied dash. 'Dimitrios is back,' Nikos said lazily, and Ria was glad of the concealing darkness to hide the sudden colour that flooded her face at the laconic words. Her heart leapt into her throat and she felt ridiculously like a fifteen-year-old schoolgirl on her first date, sick with nervous excitement.

Just for a second before Dimitrios appeared through the open lounge doors Ria had a premonition of approaching doom, drawing back behind Nikos and

Poppy as they hurried up the winding path. She heard his voice first, chiding the dogs for their exuberance, and then he stood framed in the arched doorway, his arm casually round a tall slim redhead whose tight black dress fitted where it touched- and it touched in all the right places.

'Kristie!' Nikos's shout of welcome brought Poppy to a halt, and as Ria reached her the two girls looked to where Nikos was swinging the squealing girl round and round as she protested shrilly.

'Who is this?' Poppy whispered in awe. 'Look at that hair and those legs.' Ria did look, feeling suddenly cold in the warm breeze. Whoever she was, she was on excellent terms with Dimitrios. As Nikos carried her, struggling prettily, over to where he stood, his face was smiling and relaxed as he looked down at the wriggling girl.

'Behave yourself, Nikos,' he cautioned, laughing. 'You should know by now Kristie can pack a punch!'

'Oh, you!' the girl pouted as Nikos carried her past him into the villa, leaving Dimitrios standing alone.

'Come on in and meet Kristie,' he invited, his eyes lingering on Ria's face as Poppy hurried past him, shrieks from within the house making her mouth tighten into a thin line and her back straighten. As Ria went to follow he put a restraining hand on her arm, forcing her to look at him.

'Thank you for all you've done,' he said gently. 'Christina tells me you've worked till you've dropped.'

'There's still masses to do,' Ria countered shakily, flustered by his eyes tight on her face and feeling dwarfed by his great height. She had forgotten how tall and overpoweringly masculine he was.

'We've plenty of time,' he said reassuringly, and was just about to say more, his hand tightening on her arm, when a cool female voice deliberately cut into the night, the accent very American.

'Dimitrios...darling,' it drawled, 'you haven't introduced me to your little friend,' and the redhead came slowly across the veranda towards them, her green eyes flashing in the rainbow light from the tiny lamps hung all round the top of the garden.

'Kristie, meet Ria. Ria, Kristie,' Dimitrios said formally as he drew them both into the villa.

'How do you do?' Ria smiled warily, meeting the cold green gaze head on.

'Oh, I do wonderfully, don't I, darling?' Kristie laughed, turning in mid-stride in front of Dimitrios so he was forced to catch her in his arms. 'See?' The look she threw at Ria was a challenge only another woman could understand, and Dimitrios, seemingly unaware of any undercurrents, smacked her playfully on the bottom as he pushed her gently away.

'Behave yourself, you wicked woman,' he smiled warningly, 'or I'll have to take you in hand.'

'Ooh, yes, please,' Kristie gushed sickeningly, causing Poppy's winged eyebrows to raise sharply. Catching sight of the disgusted expression on her cousin's face brought Ria momentary comfort, which vanished immediately as Kristie slipped possessive arms through the men's arms and led them into the dining area, leaving Poppy and Ria to make up the rear.

'What an old bag!' Poppy hissed viciously in Ria's ear as they trailed behind the others. 'Who is she?'

'No idea,' Ria whispered back miserably, agreeing heartily with her cousin's description but horribly aware that the redhead was quite breathtakingly beautiful in her own way. She was older than Ria had first thought, probably in her mid-thirties, but with a flawless white skin in which her green eyes were set like bright clear emeralds. The long curly red hair that fell to below her shoulders owed nothing to artifice, and her figure looked all her own too, full and curvaceous in all the right places.

Over a glass of excellent old sherry, it transpired that Kristie was a distant cousin. 'Several times removed,' she insisted with a loaded glance at Dimitrios. 'We only discovered each other a few years ago, didn't we, darling?' she purred at him, waving a languid white hand weighed down with flashing stones.

'I was in America on business,' Dimitrios explained to the two girls, looking slightly uncomfortable as Kristie sat close to him on the sofa, almost on his lap, stroking his arm now and again with light teasing fingers. 'My aunt asked me to contact Kristie; she was going through something of a bad patch,' he continued, elaborating no further.

Kristie had no such compunction. 'Oh, we're among friends, darling,' she cooed sweetly, fluttering her eyelashes at him so obviously that Poppy gave a snort of laughter against Ria's shoulder. 'What Dimitrios means is that I was going through the most ghastly divorce,' she explained directly to Ria, holding her eyes in a sharp green gaze. 'My ex was proving extremely difficult and I needed a shoulder to cry on. Dimitrios obliged.'

'I did what I could,' Dimitrios said dismissively, and Kristie looked at him, slanting her eyes provocatively.

'And you did it so well,' she purred, the innuendo so blatant that everyone shifted uncomfortably in their seats, and Dimitrios hastily urged them to the table for dinner.

'I can't stand this,' Poppy muttered in Ria's ear as Kristie monopolised the conversation all through dinner, cleverly drawing on old shared memories which totally excluded them from joining in any of the dialogue. 'She's like one of those revolting vampires from an old horror movie.'

'Well, whatever she is they aren't objecting,' Ria whispered back in despair, looking to where the two men were smiling indulgently at another of Kristie's little jokes. It was clear that the lovely American had been far more than just a friend to Dimitrios in the past, and probably still was for all she knew.

The long evening dragged to a close and, as they all stood at the bottom of the stairs saying their goodnights, Dimitrios drew Ria to one side with his back to the others. 'I've told Christina she can get up tomorrow if she is sensible,' he said quietly, and as she nodded her agreement he continued, 'I'm sorry, Ria. This evening hasn't been much fun for you, has it?'

'It's all right,' said Ria coolly, determined not to let him see how his absorption with Kristie had hurt her. 'I'm not here to have fun.'

'Kristie will settle down in a couple of days,' he said apologetically, although his eyes had hardened fractionally at her reply. 'She's just a little excited tonight. It's been a few months since she was last here and we had a bit of catching up to do.'

'Really?' Ria said facetiously, wondering in amazement if this normally astute man really was unaware of the other woman's patent hostility towards her. 'Well, it's none of my business, is it?'

She turned from his gaze, trying to

keep her face non-committal as the sugary American voice called her attention softly. 'Goodnight, Ria. I'm so glad I've met you. We must have a long chat tomorrow and get to know each other better.'

'Goodnight, Kristie,' said Ria carefully, aware of the other woman's curious glance on them both. 'I'm afraid I shall be tied up with wedding arrangements until evening but you can help if you like.'

The green eyes glinted. 'No problem.' The voice was deliberately light. 'I'm sure I can persuade Dimitrios to take a day off at any rate and keep me company. What's the use of all that money if you can't enjoy it occasionally?'

Dimitrios shook his head in refusal, his face harder than she had seen it that evening. 'No way, Kristie. I've been away a week and there's too much waiting for me. I'm sure Ria would appreciate some help, though. That goes for you too, Poppy. It's time you put in some effort.'

As Poppy flounced up the stairs, her back portraying her opinion of the whole evening, Kristie's face preserved its expression of smiling good humour with obvious effort. 'But I've only seen you for a few hours on the plane,' she protested sweetly, her voice pleading. 'You should have spared me a few hours over the last week.'

'Kristie, I was in America on business,' Dimitrios said patiently. 'I was working from seven in the morning till late at night. There was just no time.'

'OK, darling.' The older woman capitulated suddenly with a radiant smile, tucking her arm in his and pulling him towards the stairs. 'I forgive you, but you'd better make it up to me. All work and no play...' She shot Ria a look of feline cunning. 'Tell Rosa I'll have breakfast in bed tomorrow morning, would you, honey?' In the space of a few hours she has relegated me to little less than a servant, Ria thought mutinously as she delivered the required message to a clearly less than pleased Rosa. She had to hand it to the older woman, though, she had style. She had never seen anyone manipulate people so adroitly and with such ease.

The next morning set the tone for the ensuing days. Kristie drifted downstairs for breakfast in barely decent nightwear, beautifully made up, and as soon as the men had left for the plant she disappeared for the rest of the morning.

She would surface at midday to spend a little time with Christina while they ate lunch together, and then wander round the garden or house during the afternoon, reading glossy magazines and calling Rosa constantly for iced drinks. She was always immaculately dressed with not a strand of hair out of place, her eyes glittering glacially whenever they happened to rest on Ria's slight form.

Poppy and Kristie had immediately settled into an arrangement whereby they ignored each other's existence, but for some reason the older woman couldn't leave Ria alone. Her malevolent green eyes followed her every move, her barbed tongue all the more vicious when her 'helpful' suggestions were delivered in soft dulcet tones.

'I suppose you must be tremendously grateful to Dimitrios that he's allowing you to repay him a little for all his generosity,' she drawled on the first day, watching Ria as she ticked off wedding-presents on one of the lists, her smooth forehead puckered over some of the Greek names.

'What do you mean?' asked Ria calmly, inhaling a steadying deep breath and warning herself to go carefully.

Kristie leant across the back of the

202

settee where she was sprawled, flicking the ash from the long cigarette holder she held between red-tipped fingers in the general direction of the ashtray. 'Well, I can imagine how absolutely awful you feel at your little cousin's having trapped Nikos into marrying her,' the soft voice taunted spitefully. 'And then to stay on here for an extended holiday week after week...'

It was so far from the truth that Ria stared dumbly at the beautiful cold face before her. 'It's not like that at all,' she said at last, her voice stiff. 'Nikos and Poppy are in love and Dimitrios asked me to stay to help.'

'Oh, really?' Kristie gave a tight derogatory laugh and turned back to the pages of her magazine, flicking the pages in irritating idleness.

The evenings were even less bearable. As soon as Dimitrios returned Kristie would wrap herself round him like a clinging plant, sighing dramatically with exhaustion, her catlike eyes daring the cousins to contradict her. Ria found herself avoiding Dimitrios whenever she could after that first evening, disappearing to her room as soon as dinner was over and waiting until she heard his car leave in the morning before she came down to breakfast. A protecting numbness had settled over her mind since his return. The first night she had cried herself to sleep but now she seemed to be existing in a kind of limbo, aware she was playing directly into Kristie's hands but unable to react.

She didn't think he had noticed, but on the fourth night as she was preparing for bed she heard a gentle tap at her door. Thinking it was Rosa with the milky bedtime drink Christina now insisted she had, declaring she was losing too much weight, she shrugged a short bathrobe over her naked body and padded to the door, opening it to find Dimitrios standing with his hands resting on lean hips, his stance arrogant and his mouth ominously tight.

'I want a word with you.' He brushed past her into the room and Ria caught a whiff of Kristie's heavy cloying perfume on his clothes as she shut the door.

'Well?' He stood facing her, dark and intimidating, arms crossed and eyes narrowed. 'Are you going to tell me what is going on or do I have to drag it out of you?'

'I don't know what you're talking about,' Ria lied defiantly, the nauseating perfume teasing her nostrils and making her stomach muscles clench.

'Really?' The steel-blue eyes snapped furiously as they encompassed the slight, hostile little figure standing with back straight and small chin jutting out. 'I suppose I'm imagining it, then?' His gaze hardened still further at her silence. 'Look, young lady, I'm not leaving this room until I find out why you scuttle away like a frightened rabbit every time you see me.'

Ria's gaze, turned fiery at the unflattering simile. 'Kristie has intimated that the workload is too much for you. Is that true?'

'No, it is not,' Ria denied angrily, 'and she can keep her opinions to herself.'

'For crying out loud!' He ran a hand through his black hair. 'She was only trying to help.'

'Well, that's the first time she has helped since she's been here, then!' As soon as she said the words she knew she was condemning herself further in his eyes, she had sounded so petty.

'Now look, something is eating you up and I want to know what it is.' He was clearly hanging on to his patience by a thread, his voice brusque. 'When I went away I thought we were getting on fine, and I come back...'

His cool reference to that shared time that she had pinned so many hopes on suddenly took all the fight out of her. She would rather die than tell him it was tearing her apart to see him with Kristie, she would never give him that satisfaction.

'I'm perfectly all right.' Her voice was cold. 'Just because I don't want to spend every minute in your company doesn't make me abnormal, you know. You're not irresistible, whatever you may think.'

'I don't believe I'm having this conversation!' His voice was very angry and mildly perplexed. 'Whoever said anything about spending every minute with me?'

'Well, you certainly didn't,' Ria snapped back illogically. She knew she wasn't making sense but she was past caring. 'And I wouldn't want to if you did!'

'Wouldn't you?' His mouth formed a grim line and before she could ascertain his intention he had pulled her into his arms and taken possession of her mouth in a hard hungry kiss. She was immobile for a brief moment and then red-hot rage enveloped her. No! It wasn't going to happen again. How dared he think he could pay her the minimum of attention for days and then she would just fall into his arms in grateful submission when he deigned to recognise her existence again?

She kicked out suddenly with her legs, feeling him wince as her foot made contact with his shin-bone, and as he tightened his hold on her she struggled and fought against his hard body, beating her fists against the iron muscles of his back. His mouth was now ravaging hers in a form of cruel punishment and she could taste blood on her lips.

'She wasn't aware the robe had fallen open until he pushed her backwards on to the soft covers of the bed, kneeling above her, his breathing ragged and uneven, holding her slim arms over her head in a relentless grip. As his burning eyes swept down the length of her body spread out before him she closed her eyes to shut out what was happening. A solitary tear escaped from her swimming eyes and slid down her face but she made no sound, determined not to complete the humiliation by begging for release.

Seconds ticked by and then he made an anguished sound deep in his throat and her aching arms were free. She curled into a little ball to protect herself from his gaze, eyes still tightly shut, and then she felt his finger touch the wetness on her face.

'What are you doing to me?' he, whispered huskily, self-loathing contorting the words until she could hardly understand what he was saying. He folded the robe round her body, drawing her upwards until she was sitting pressed against his chest, his heartbeat deafening against her ear. Embarrassment and fright kept her rigid against his body, and after a moment he stood up, his tortured glance grimly assessing the stark whiteness of her face and the bruised swelling of her trembling lips.

'I won't insult you by asking you to forgive such conduct,' he said slowly, his voice raw. 'I can only say I am deeply sorry and promise you it will never happen again. If you feel you must go back to England immediately I will arrange for you to leave tomorrow.'

She kept her head lowered and her eyes shut as she replied. 'I will stay until the wedding. I keep my word.' As she heard the door close she opened her eyes to the empty room and it reflected the great void in her heart where her love for him had been. She would never forgive him, never.

The next day Christina made no comment when she saw her swollen lips and the deep violet shadows under her eyes that no amount of make-up would disguise, but Ria could feel her concerned gaze as they went through the catering lists together.

She had learnt at breakfast that Dimitrios had left early that morning on a two-day trip to one of the islands, taking Kristie with him. 'Sudden decision,' Nikos had explained briefly, his face stiff with disapproval, and Poppy had reached over and taken Ria's hand in her own, her face deeply troubled. It warmed Ria's frozen heart slightly to know they were concerned about her, but the events of the night before were so vivid in her mind that she couldn't concentrate on anything for long. There had been a dead hopeless sound to his voice as he had left her room that hadn't registered until much later. All her hopes and dreams lay in fragments around her and she didn't even have the strength to care any more. She welcomed this numbness that seemed to have claimed her senses, drawing it to her and resting in its anaesthetising comfort.

'A trouble shared is a trouble halved,' said Christina as they finished the last list, a look of compassion softening the drawn face. Ria looked at her blankly. She didn't want to talk to Christina, didn't want to do anything that might melt this ice from around her heart and make her feel again.

'Come on, Ria,' Christina's voice persuaded gently. 'I might be locked away in this room most of the time but I'm not blind. You haven't been yourself since Kristie came. Is she being difficult?'

The concern in Christina's voice was her undoing. As her eyes began to mist treacherously she stumbled to her feet, intending to leave the room, but the older woman stood up too, putting a comforting arm round her shoulders and leading her over to the balcony where Rosa had recently left a mid-morning snack.

'Right, let's get to the bottom of all this,' Christina said briskly when she had poured them both a steaming cup of coffee and made Ria take a few sips. 'You musn't let Kristie get under your skin, my dear. She's the same with any attractive unattached female under the age of sixty. It isn't you personally.'

'It's not just her.' Ria felt unable to elaborate in the face of Christina's kindness.

'Dimitrios?' asked the other woman ruefully, and as Ria's startled gaze met the vivid blue eyes Christina shook her head gently. 'He's rushing you, I suppose; patience never was his strong point even as a child.'

'Rushing me?'

'Well, you know how he feels about you, surely?' Christina was plainly exasperated but Ria had no idea where this muddled conversation was leading, and her confusion was mirrored in the wide grey eyes for the older woman to read. 'You must know he cares deeply for you?' asked Christina in amazement. 'Haven't you noticed the way his whole face changes the moment he lays eyes on you? No, perhaps you haven't,' she pondered thoughtfully as her eyes rested on Ria's blank face.

'You've got it all wrong,' Ria began anxiously. 'He hasn't bothered with me at all since Kristie has been here and now he's taken her along with him on this trip. There are times when I think he actually hates me.' Her lower lip quivered as she fought for control.

'Hate is the sister of love,' Christina said drily. 'It's easy to mistake one for the other.'

'Dimitrios doesn't love me,' Ria protested sadly. 'I don't think he even likes me. He's attracted to me physically because I look so much like Caroline but every time we're together we seem to fight.'

'And you?' Christina watched her face closely. 'How do you feel?'

The colour came and went in Ria's pale face as she looked into the eyes so like Dimitrios's. It would be so comforting to share her burden with someone, someone she could trust. 'I love him very much,' she stammered at last, hearing her voice say the words out loud with a little twinge of fear. 'But please don't tell him. It would only embarrass and annoy him and I don't want his pity.'

'I certainly won't tell him,' Christina affirmed sharply, 'because you are going to as soon as he returns.'

'I can't,' whispered Ria miserably, her eyes stricken. 'Don't you see, Christina? He's taken Kristie with him on this trip, just the two of them, alone. I hardly think that is the action of a man in love.'

'How do you know he's gone alone with her?' Christina asked forcefully. 'Did he tell you that?'

'Well, no,' Ria admitted shakily. 'I just assumed...'

'There's been a bit too much assuming all round, if you ask me,' Christina said firmly, sounding very English. 'Add to that a little touch of Kristie and it's asking for trouble. Believe me, Ria, if he'd wanted her he could have had her years ago. I won't say they weren't more than friends at first but he quickly lost interest. Unfortunately Kristie is as tenacious as an octopus once she has her tentacles round something. It's a family trait, I'm afraid.' Her voice was wry.

A glimmer of hope raised its head. 'I've tried to hate him,' Ria whispered brokenly, 'but it's no good. Even when he's...' She shook her head. 'I still love him.'

'Then tell him. He's a very proud man, Ria, and he has been hurt badly once; he won't make the mistake of wearing his heart on his sleeve twice. You've got to make him understand how you really feel.'

'I don't think I can,' she said quietly.

Christina looked at her long and hard. 'That's for you to decide. It really depends on how much you want him, doesn't it?'

The rest of the day dragged interminably. By evening she was exhausted with the thoughts raging in her head and, forgoing dinner, she stumbled to her room, falling into a deep dreamless sleep as soon as her head touched the pillow The next day found her rested and more able to cope, but as the day progressed a restless nervous tension gripped her, limiting her concentration and accelerating her heartbeat in bursts of tingling energy. She went for a long walk in the late afternoon, returning to the harbour where the brightly painted fishing-boats were slumbering in the evening sun at dusk as mauve shadows began to creep their fingers over the still water.

She walked back through the garden —the dusky air was spiced with the perfume of wild roses and honeysuckle that grew in the crevices of the old sun-drenched wall, and a solitary songbird sent its sweetly piercing voice flooding out into the darkening sky as she stood quietly listening, head on one side.

'I thought I'd find you here.' The

American voice held a faintly mocking note as Ria turned sharply to see Kristie sauntering down the path, her pale skin glowing pearly white in the shadows.

'Yes?' Unknowingly Ria lifted her small chin proudly and squared her back as though for battle. The subtle body language was not lost on Kristie's sharp cool eyes and a small smile touched the edge of her painted mouth.

'Dimitrios informs me you'll be leaving immediately after the wedding? Someone waiting for you in England?' Ria shrugged a non-committal reply; Kristie's forced friendly tones were jarring on her nerves.

Kristie lowered painted lids over her slanted eyes, their expression hidden from Ria as she trailed a limp hand along the rough stone of the wall, plucking a small flower from its depths and then crushing it thoughtlessly in her fingers. 'It's just that I've got some news I know you'll be thrilled to hear but you'll miss it if you dash off. It's a secret for the time being, you see.'

'Why share it with me if it's a secret?', Ria said stiffly, a sense of impending doom sending a shiver of apprehension down her spine. Kristie's face had a gloating look about it that she couldn't define.

The redhead's small full lips pouted prettily. 'I know you'll think I'm awful but I must tell someone and, anyway, it wouldn't be fair for you to be the last to know. You'll sort of be a distant member of the family after your cousin marries Nikos, won't you?' She smiled at Ria, raising her eyes, and Ria caught a glimpse of the razor-sharp green gaze before it was swiftly veiled by long mascaraed lashes.

'Dimitrios is adamant we must keep the announcement until after the wedding, you know—in case any of the glory is taken away from the happy couple!'

'Announcement?' Fortifying pride kept her voice steady but her face was white as she stared at the smiling woman in front of her.

'I can tell you've guessed already.' Kristie laughed lightly, opening her eyes wide in an innocent gaze. 'Dimitrios asked me today to be his wife.' Ria stared disbelievingly at the older woman, and as she went to speak Kristie thrust a small box under her nose, clicking open the top to reveal a magnificent ring nestling inside.

'Beautiful, isn't it?' Kristie said softly, and as Ria stared at the huge emerald surrounded by a star of diamonds her heart froze. 'Of course everyone has known for years we would get married one day,' Kristie whispered, 'but Dimitrios needed to get the business into a position where he could let it run itself for a few years while we start a family. Still, we decided today we can't wait for ever.'

Kristie looked hard at her white shocked face and, obviously satisfied with the reaction her news had had, she began to teeter up the uneven path again on her outlandishly high heels, tucking the box back in the pocket of her silk jacket. 'Don't forget, not a word now. I'd hate to be the one to spoil things for Poppy.'

Left alone, Ria groped blindly for the nearest seat, staring into the shadows in stunned misery. Christina had been wrong, after all; she should have known, it would have been too good to be true. What would a man like him want with a little nobody like her? For a few moments her self-esteem drained into the deep abyss Kristie had created and then her sense of self-worth asserted itself again and she clawed her way out of the mindless pit. She wouldn't let this destroy her. She would smile, and talk, and socialise for the next few days until she could go home to England and lick her wounds in peace. She had survived before she met Dimitrios and she would after he was gone. They wouldn't beat her.

CHAPTER EIGHT

'Hello, Ria.' The voice was as she remembered, deep and vibrant, but there was no life in those sky-blue eyes as they met her own; Dimitrios could have been looking at a stranger. It was the final death-knell of any hope she had had left.

She had walked up the dark garden and into the bright lights of the house as though in a dream, really only coming to herself as Poppy had called out to her as she had stepped through the big doors to join the others as they sat in the lounge having pre-dinner drinks. Her cousin's perceptive eyes had narrowed at her pale face, but her gaze was riveted on the big dark figure next to Kristie on one of the sofas, his face remote and cold.

'Did you have a good trip?' she asked carefully, keeping her face blank by supreme effort. She had noticed the possessive arm linked in his and the way Kristie was curled into his side like a sleek, well-fed cat.

219

'Productive,' he said easily, turning his head down to Kristie as she whispered something in his ear. Poppy and Nikos shifted uncomfortably from their position across the room, and everyone seemed faintly relieved when Christina joined them and they started dinner.

'Dimitrios didn't go with her alone, you know,' Poppy began as she walked up the winding staircase with Ria on their way to bed later that night. 'Nikos asked him specifically and apparently he just gave her a lift there and back to do some shopping, and there were two other men with him the whole time. He didn't even stay at the same hotel as her and—'

'It doesn't matter.' Ria's voice was dead and after one quick darting glance at her cousin's white face Poppy was quiet. He hadn't even looked at her all evening unless he was forced to do so, and then those steel-blue eyes had been empty and blank, devoid of even that gleam of desire that had burnt in their depths before.

Alone in her room she kicked off the low-heeled sandals she was wearing and padded out on to the warm floor of the balcony. Her head was aching fiercely and she felt drained of all feeling; she had acted her way through the evening with magnificent fervour and now it was taking its toll.

She sat there in the rich darkness in a quiet daze, feeling the tension and exhaustion seep out of her in great flowing waves, the air cool and comforting on her burning forehead. She heard a small movement on the veranda below, the noise loud in the stillness of the sleeping night. It was Dimitrios, she knew. She kept quite still, hardly breathing, sensing he knew she was there.

After a timeless age she heard him call the dogs gruffly, his voice curt, and then a few minutes later the Land Rover roared off into the night. So he couldn't sleep either. The thought brought her some comfort, although she wasn't sure why, and eventually she went to bed, lying awake for hours in the scented darkness until sleep claimed her tortured mind.

There was a telegram for Kristie the next morning at breakfast and as she read it her lips tightened into a thin red line. 'Damn and blast!'

'Problems?' Dimitrios raised uninterested eyes from behind the newspaper he was reading, and she looked at him sweetly, composing her face into a soft smile.

'Just Mother having one of her little turns again. She expects me to drop everything wherever I am and fly to her side at a moment's notice.' A vitriolic note had crept into her voice and at Dimitrios's raised eyebrows she flushed slightly, green eyes wary.

'I wasn't aware Joan was having health problems.' Christina's voice was concerned and her gaze was sharp as she looked at the lovely redhead, who was sitting sulkily crumbling a small roll between long manicured fingers.

'Oh, you know Mother. One thing after another.' Kristie's voice was working on being offhand. 'The latest is angina and now they've found there is a leaking valve to her heart. It isn't serious but she expects—'

'Kristie!' Christina's voice was splinter-cold. 'In all the time that I have known your Mother she has never complained of her health once. If she needs you now you leave on the first available plane. Arrange it, please, Dimitrios.' Dimitrios saluted in mock obedience, his eyes laughing at his sister.

Kristie slumped back in her seat, her face red with rage and quite ugly for a brief second, and Dimitrios shot her a cool glance as she went to open her mouth again. 'You go today, Kristie.' His voice brooked no argument and the redhead looked utterly deflated. Ria almost had it in her to feel sorry...almost.

'That's shot her bolt for a while,' Poppy said with great satisfaction as they watched Nikos drive her off to the airport later that morning. 'She really is an old cow!'

'Poppy!' Ria's voice was reprimanding but there was laughter tinging the shock. Anyone less like a cow than the elegant redhead she couldn't imagine.

'Not the words I would have chosen but the sentiment I agree with.' Christina's dry voice made the two girls jump, and the older woman beckoned to Ria to join her on the veranda, dismissing Poppy with regal indifference. The relationship between Christina and her future daughter-in-law was less than perfect, Ria mused as she followed the stooped figure out into the warm air; she could only hope it would get better with time.

'Have you talked to Dimitrios?' Christina asked quietly when they were seated, and

Ria shook her head wearily.

'No. I've decided not to.'

The silence deepened as Christina, watched her downcast face intently. 'May I ask why?' she said at last.

'I've decided it wouldn't work,' Ria said flatly, her eyes lowered and her cheeks flushing as she felt Christina's disapproval. 'I see.'

'There's so much against us and I don't feel I can give the relationship what it would need to work,' Ria said unhappily, hating to lie but unable to tell Dimitrios's sister the truth. She couldn't tell her her brother was engaged to be married before he did.

'I disagree, but of course it is your choice.' Christina's voice was colder than it had ever been with her before, and Ria raised brimming eyes suddenly, catching hold of the older woman's hands pleadingly.

'Please, Christina. Nothing has changed, I do love him very much but I just can't...'

'But why not?' Christina's demeanour changed as she saw her distress, and she put an arm protectively round her shoulders. 'No, I won't ask you any more.

I'm sorry, Ria. It's just that I would so love you to become a member of my family; I'm very fond of you, you know, and you would be so right for my brother. But I mustn't press you. I forget sometimes how young you are.'

She wiped Ria's eyes with a soft lace handkerchief, her touch gentle. 'We won't mention it again, my dear, but if ever you need a friend you know I am here.'

'Thank you.' This made it all so much worse, Ria thought despairingly. Would this torment never end?

With Kristie gone the atmosphere of the house improved during the day, although once Dimitrios was home everyone seemed on tenterhooks. He was working almost twenty hours a day, arriving back at the villa just in time for dinner each evening, his handsome face drawn and cold, his eyes chips of blue ice. He would sit in morose silence while they ate uncomfortably and then disappear immediately into his study with a briefcase of papers, working into the early hours. On the rare occasions when she caught his glance his face appalled her with its darkness, a black emotion emanating from him that chilled her veins.

They were having breakfast on the sunlit

veranda one morning, the wedding now only a week away, when Nikos turned to Poppy apologetically. There were only the three of them sitting in companionable silence. Christina wasn't feeling too well and had asked for a tray in her room and Dimitrios had eaten earlier, so Rosa informed them, and had taken the dogs out for a walk before the heat of the day rendered them immobile.

Nikos was rapidly spooning a delicious concoction of Rosa's into his mouth, small ripe balls of fruit marinated overnight in red wine and syrup, when he clasped his hand to his head in dismay. 'I forgot to tell you, Poppy, I shan't be back tonight till late, so don't expect us for dinner.'

'Why?' Poppy's voice was truculent. 'The days are long enough as it is with you gone.'

'I can't help it,' Nikos said placatingly. 'Dimitrios is giving me a month off when we get married and, besides, you'll be by yourself all day then when I go off to work each morning.'

'That will be quite different and you know it.' Poppy wasn't going to be mollified. 'Why are you going to be late?'

'There's a function at the plant tonight,'

Nikos said uncomfortably, obviously aware that his volatile fiancée was not going to like what she heard. 'Dimitrios has been working on a deal for some months with the American contingent and they've sent out a scout team to map out the land. We thought it would be good company relations to hold a barbecue in the grounds tonight for our employees and their families. The Americans like things like that,' he finished weakly as Poppy leapt to her feet visibly bristling, her auburn curls bobbing angrily in the bright sunlight.

'You pig!' she said, her eyes flashing. 'What am I if I'm not your family? And Ria's *my* family, so why weren't we invited?'

'You weren't invited because I told Nikos not to mention the event to you.' The cold hard voice bit through the air and the three of them froze, looking down the garden to where Dimitrios had just entered the small gate. Ria's heart jumped at the sight of him; his shirt was unbuttoned at the throat and the casual trousers that he wore revealed each muscled leg in detailed outline, moulded by the dampness of the sea spray against his long strong legs. His eyes were glittering as he walked up to where they sat, looking directly at Poppy as she stood her ground determinedly.

'Why?' She tossed her head as she spoke, injured self-pity colouring her voice. 'Why can't I come?'

'This is work for Nikos and me, Poppy, not some nice social gathering when he can attend to your whims and fancies.' He was clearly in the grip of a filthy mood.

'I don't want Nikos to look after me, thank you very much!' Poppy replied stubbornly. 'I'm quite capable of looking after myself.'

'I don't doubt that for a minute.' The deep voice was lethal and now Nikos rose in protest.

'Hang on a second, Dimitrios.'

'As for you!' Dimitrios swung round on his nephew with quiet venom. 'I told you not to mention it to her in the first place; why can't you do as you're told for once?'

Ria sat aghast as the three of them faced each other like warriors preparing to do battle. The unpleasantness had blown up so quickly that it had left her stunned but now a niggling little thought crept into her head. Was the reason Dimitrios didn't want Poppy along that she might come too?

'If you're worried about me bothering Nikos I won't even talk to him all night.' Poppy clearly believed attack was the best weapon. 'Ria will keep me company and we can look after each other. Please, Nikos,' she turned to her fiancé imploringly, turning her eyes into melting pools, 'I haven't been out in ages and I shan't be able to wear nice clothes much longer and dress up.'

'Dimitrios?' Nikos turned to his uncle with a plea on his young face, and Dimitrios swore softly, his eyes on Poppy.

'You can turn off the spaniel approach with me,' he said coldly, 'I'm immune. If you want to come, come. Don't expect to enjoy yourself and you'll have to wait until we've finished before you can come home whether you're tired or not.'

He strode off into the house with a last furious look at his nephew and Poppy settled back in her seat, quite unperturbed by all the drama. In fact, thought Ria, looking at her cousin's satisfied face, she looked as though she had thoroughly enjoyed that. Poppy's next words confirmed it. 'Well, I've had more gracious invitations before, but that will have to do,' she said complacently, flashing a quick grin at Ria and turning an innocent face up to Nikos, who was still standing looking bewilderedly after his uncle. She could handle Dimitrios far better than me, Ria thought wistfully, a small thread of envy in her eyes at Poppy's total lack of concern.

'You'll come, won't you, Ria?' Poppy said suddenly, obviously remembering she hadn't even asked her cousin if she wanted to go.

'I can't refuse after all that, can I?' Ria said drily, her voice cool but a spark of amusement in her eyes. She couldn't hide the stirring of admiration she felt for her cousin's single-mindedness. There were times when she wished there were a grain of that in her make-up.

Looking through the limited wardrobe she had with her later that day, she realised she had no idea what to wear. All the barbecues she attended in England were neighbourly affairs with jeans and T-shirts being common uniform, but it was different out here. Eventually she decided on a black silk sundress she had had for ages but still felt good in. The close-fitting waist and full swirling hemline flattered her slim figure and she needed every bit of confidence she could dredge up tonight.

She brushed her long hair till it gleamed, leaving it loose so that it floated round her shoulders in a pale silver sheen making her large grey eyes seem enormous by contrast. She only needed a touch of peach lipstick—days in the sun had given her smooth skin a golden glow that cosmetics couldn't enhance—and after a faint stroking of mascara on her thick dark lashes she was ready, her black patent sandals clicking nervously as she walked down the long staircase.

'Wow!' Poppy was waiting for her downstairs looking young and pretty in a pale lemon dress with matching shoes, and she whistled admiringly at her cousin, brown eyes sparkling.

'You're going to knock them dead tonight, baby,' she said delightedly. 'If this doesn't make Dimitrios sit up and take notice nothing will!'

'Poppy.' Ria's voice held a warning and her cousin held up a conciliatory hand.

'All right, all right. I can't understand him, though. Mind you, I can't understand you either. Why you want him is beyond me. He scares me to death, he's so cold and—'

She stopped as Ria turned round and

prepared to walk back up the stairs, her face stony.

'I promise, I promise. Not another word about him shall darken my wicked lips.' Laughing now, Ria let herself be persuaded back to wait for the taxi that was to take them to the plant.

The barbecue was in full swing when they arrived and after quickly introducing them to a few people Nikos disappeared into the throng, leaving them standing uncertainly on the outskirts of the crowd, glass of wine in hand. At first it seemed as though hundreds of people were milling about on the large lawn at the back of the office buildings, but after a few minutes they realised there were about sixty to seventy adults with a large number of children of varying ages, all extremely well dressed and beautifully behaved.

Dusk was falling rapidly, its shadows banished to the outskirts of the grass by the rainbow light of hundreds of small glass lanterns swinging in the cool evening air. Poppy was deep in animated conversation with a young, heavily pregnant American woman and Ria stood to one side of a small group, her face pensive and her thoughts far away.

'Hey, Ria, honey, is it really you?' a warm American voice drawled, and as she raised startled eyes the tall blond man in front of her let out a whoop of delight.

'Frank!' As she spoke his name he enveloped her in a huge bear-hug, easily lifting her off the ground in strong young arms and swinging her round madly until she begged for mercy, her silky hair covering both their faces.

'What are you doing here?' they both exclaimed at the same moment and then collapsed against each other, laughing, his arms still round her in a friendly hug, unaware of a tall dark figure watching them carefully over the heads of the crowd, impervious to the gaiety surrounding him.

'You look absolutely delicious, honey-pot,' Frank began, a wide grin lighting up his attractive face. 'Where have you been hiding for the last few weeks?'

'I haven't been hiding,' she protested, a warm flush colouring her cheeks as his light blue eyes swept admiringly over her body from head to toe. 'I'm here with Poppy. She's engaged to Nikos and they're getting married in a few days, so I've had something of an extended holiday. Do you know him?'

'Sure I know him. We've been doing business with his uncle most of the time but Nikos has sat in on a few of the discussions. He's a nice lad.' Ria smiled at the terminology. Frank could only be a few years older than Nikos and he was talking as though he were Methuselah.

'I wish I'd known you were here,' Frank continued ruefully. 'We go home tomorrow.' Ria looked at his pleasant uncomplicated face and spontaneously gave him a light kiss on his cheek. His pleasure at seeing her was a healing balm to her sore heart and she had always liked Frank. She had met him just before she gave up modelling, when she had engaged in a series of swimwear promotions, and he had been immediately bowled over by her cool blonde beauty, attending every function she worked and dogging her footsteps hopefully until she was forced to tell him gently that he was a friend, nothing more.

'When am I going to persuade you on another date?' he asked now, never one to miss an opportunity and she smiled sadly up into his eyes, putting a finger on his mouth reproachfully.

'Don't start that again,' she said mildly, wishing in that moment that she had been able to love him instead of giving her heart to a man who seemed to take pleasure in trampling it underfoot.

'I can't help it,' he said half laughing, half serious, his eyes warm on her face. 'I want to devour you—'

'Try the barbecue, Frank, it's less likely to give you indigestion.' As the cool barbed words cut in on the young American's voice they both swung round, Ria's face apprehensive and Frank's slightly startled at the coolly insulting expression on Dimitrios's unsmiling face.

'You know each other?' he continued. For some reason Ria sensed he was furiously angry although he appeared his cold, nonchalant self, hands thrust deep into the pockets of his tailored grey trousers as his eyes flicked over their joined arms.

'Sure do,' Frank affirmed, his eyes slightly puzzled. 'This little lady is an old friend, although the last time I saw you you were only half dressed,' he joked in an aside to Ria, his attempt to lighten the heavy atmosphere falling like a stone into the sudden silence.

'Meaning what?' Dimitrios's narrowed eyes were brilliant with anger and he had never looked more dangerous. She thought

235

for a moment that he was going to hit the other man and Frank obviously did too, as they moved closer together like combatants in a boxing ring.

'Dimitrios!' She inserted her slim body between them, looking up into the dark grim face and holding on to his arms restrainingly. 'Please, Dimitrios, he was only joking.'

'That's no joke.' The words were sharp and furious, causing a few interested heads to turn their way and conversation to become muted. Ria could see Poppy fluttering on the outskirts of one group and hoped she would have the sense to stay well out of things for once.

'You're right.' Frank was equally grim-faced now. 'It was probably in poor taste but I thought if you knew Ria it couldn't be misconstrued.'

'It has been. Explain.'

Frank opened his mouth and then closed it again, clearly discomfited and out of his depth. Before he had found the words he was searching for, Ria spoke rapidly and quietly, still holding on to Dimitrios's taut-muscled arms with all her strength, terrified to relax her hold.

'We first met when I was modelling

swimwear in England two years ago. The last time he was in London he suggested we had a day by one of his friends' private pool, for old times' sake if you like. It just struck us funny at the time that I wore one of the costumes I had modelled when he first saw me. That's all.'

'Is it?' The question was directed straight at Frank and he answered in the same vein.

'That about sums it up, but if you're asking me if I'm interested in Ria the answer is yes, damn interested! Unfortunately up to the present time the feeling hasn't been reciprocated, but I'm working on it.'

Ria had to give him full marks for courage. He was about six inches smaller and two stones lighter than his adversary and Dimitrios towered over him, his enormous height dwarfing the young American but clearly not intimidating him.

Neither man moved for a few moments, their eyes locked in some private duel that they both understood. As Dimitrios became aware of the interest they were arousing he relaxed suddenly, drawing a deep harsh breath and taking a step backwards so that

Ria relaxed her hold on him and moved to one side. 'That of course is your privilege,' he said quietly, his face unreadable. 'We've known each other a long time, Frank; I wouldn't want to part on a sour note.'

'Likewise.' Frank's voice was dry but his gaze was perceptive as he stretched out his hand to the other man, and as Dimitrios clasped it in his own some private communication seemed to flash between them.

'I've waited a long time to see this,' Frank said in an undertone, seemingly into the air, and as a dark flush stained Dimitrios's face he smiled sardonically and turned to Ria in a brief farewell. 'Be good, honey-pot,' he said gently, his eyes wistful.

As the tall blond figure melted into the crowd the swell of conversation flowed freely again, and as Ria opened her mouth to speak into the strained silence Dimitrios took her arm, his finger on her lips.

'In a moment I am going to lead you over to a seat and you are going to sit quietly on it,' he said, his voice scathing. 'You will not move from that seat, not even if the ground erupts and the sky falls in. You will not, I repeat not, talk to any more of my guests and you will keep absolutely silent.'

She bit back an angry retort painfully, aware that some dark force stronger than himself had him in its grip and provocation could be the last straw.

'You are being totally unreasonable,' she hissed in a quiet undertone as he led her, like a guard with a prisoner, through the buzzing crowd that seemed to part magically before them. 'I haven't done anything wrong, for goodness' sake. Frank saw me and just came over to chat; you're the one who blew everything out of proportion. I didn't even know he'd be here, did I?'

'Have you quite finished?' His grip on her arm was brutal and his voice was still tight with some fierce emotion that caused a muscle in his cheek to jerk warningly. 'You seem unaware that you were making a spectacle of yourself in front of my workforce.'

Ria gasped in disbelief at the unfairness of the accusation, but as she went to stop to gather her protest he tightened his fingers until they were like steel, biting into her flesh until she could hardly bear it. 'You're hurting me,' she said weakly as he pulled her along towards a more secluded part of the lawn, where some easy-chairs had been put under the branches of an old cedar tree to provide shade in the late afternoon, not needed now darkness had fallen.

'Believe me, this is nothing to what I would like to do,' he replied woodenly, his body straight as a ramrod. 'Now sit down and don't move until I return. Have you eaten?'

'What?' She looked up at him warily, thinking she must have misheard him.

'I said, have you eaten?' He spaced the words out as though he were talking to a young and irritating child.

'No, I have not eaten,' replied Ria in the same sarcastic tone, and something gleamed in the angry blue eyes for a moment and then was swiftly veiled.

'Don't push your luck,' he said briefly as he turned away. 'Sit tight and I'll be back in a minute.'

When he returned a few moments later he was carrying a tray on which two heaped plates loaded with spiced chicken, beef, ham, green salad and small baked potatoes reposed. Next to them was an uncorked bottle of wine and two glasses, and Ria noticed with relief that his face was less forbidding.

'Right, eat that,' he said abruptly, spreading out a large napkin on her lap and passing her one of the plates with a knife and fork. He positioned a glass of wine at her feet and settled himself into a chair at her side, so close that she could smell the spicy tang of his aftershave. The warm intimacy of their solitude surrounded them subtly, and Ria felt a lump in her throat as she tried to swallow a forkful of ham.

Stop it, you idiot, she told herself firmly, he's engaged to someone else. He seemed quite relaxed and was clearly enjoying his meal, his eyes on a display of traditional Greek dancers in the distance, their bright costumes and spirited steps gathering a large crowd around the small stage on which they were performing.

'I said eat it; you're getting too thin.' He hadn't glanced at her as he spoke and she flushed at the quiet criticism. She knew she had lost a few pounds in the past few weeks but it was his fault anyway.

'You aren't my father, you know!' The retort sprang out of her mouth before she could check it and she glanced quickly at him to see his reaction. Why couldn't she think before she spoke?

'I know that.' His voice was heavy with irony and something else. 'Believe me, Ria, the feelings I have for you aren't in the least paternal.'

'Yes, well...' She was floundering and he knew it; his eyes were bright on her red face with a touch of laughter in their depths. 'I thought you were supposed to circulate?' She said the first thing that came into her mouth and his lips tightened, the light dying from his eyes.

'I presume I am allowed to finish my meal, or is my presence so repugnant to you that you would like me to leave immediately?' he said coldly.

She flinched at the icy tones but managed to reply evenly, 'I didn't mean it the way it sounded. It was just that you were so definite that Poppy and I would have to look after ourselves if we came. It was obvious you didn't want us along.'

'And how right I was,' he said with a curious intensity, his eyes sharp on her pale face.

'I thought the evening was very important as a public relations exercise,' she stammered, trying to hide the hurt his cool words had brought to her eyes.

'There are some things which are more important,' he replied ambiguously. 'Besides, if public relations is going to clinch this deal I think I've blown that, don't you?'

She flushed miserably and he lifted her chin up slowly, his hand gentle. 'Don't worry,' he said softly, 'I'm a big boy now.'

As always his touch turned her bones to water and she drew back instinctively, frightened his experience would recognise her weakness.

'Eat!' His tone brooked no argument; he had clearly mistaken the reason for her reaction, a fact that was confirmed by his next words.

'Stop looking at me as though I'm going to rape you at any moment,' he growled furiously. 'You are quite safe here, I can assure you. I'm sure the illustrious Frank would leap to your rescue if I tried to have my wicked way with you.' Ria flushed scarlet, his words conjuring up memories she would prefer to forget, and he laughed sarcastically. 'At least I can still make you do that,' he said, touching her hot cheek lightly with his forefinger.

Her skin tingled long after he had resumed eating, his face sombre, and as they ate she marvelled again at his power over her. In spite of the knowledge that he was just playing with her, that he was already committed to another woman, she couldn't resist him. It made her feel bitter as well as frightened and she didn't like the feeling, didn't like the person she could feel herself changing into. She must get away from Greece as soon as she could and never, never return.

CHAPTER NINE

'Are you still frightened of me?' They had been sitting for some time in tense silence, having finished their meal—although Ria's plate was still half full—and were sipping their second glass of wine slowly. 'I'm not some sort of monster, you know, just a man who makes mistakes occasionally, human just like you.'

Ria looked at his austere face thrown into relief by the moonlight and noticed that his mouth was curiously white, while his eyes gleamed strangely as though a fire was being studiously banked down behind their blue depths.

'I'm not frightened of you,' she lied, holding her chin up proudly, and he smiled thoughtfully, leaning forward with one leg crossed over his knee.

'Very impressive.' The words were dry and cold. 'However, on this occasion I remain unconvinced. Amazing, really, when one thinks about how you fooled me in the past.'

'You've never let me explain why I acted as I did, have you? I don't think you want to understand my motives.'

'Very possibly,' he said arrogantly. 'I've learnt it's better to rely on my judgement in such matters.'

'Or lack of it.' Ria knew she was provoking a confrontation, but the little needle of hurt pride and anger was pricking at her insidiously, making her unable to keep quiet. 'Sometimes I don't think you've got a heart at all where I'm concerned.'

'I see.' His voice was silky but dark colour flared in his high cheekbones. 'Be careful. You might not enjoy it if I respond to your challenge.' He leant forward until his breath was warm on her face, his eyes cold slits in the moonlight. 'I apologised for my actions in your room that night; I had hoped you would be able to put it behind you. Nevertheless, I am aware my actions were unforgivable.' His accent was very pronounced.

'I have put it behind me.' The words hung in the air with a ring of truth that he recognised.

'Then what is it?' he asked, his voice icy. 'I get the impression you are angry with me. You have been unapproachable ever since I returned from the American trip.'

'Perhaps I just don't like you.' She had to make him stop asking all these questions before she blurted out that he had broken her heart and crushed her fragile dreams, that she knew about Kristie and their plans for a life together. He remained perfectly still, his dark face inscrutable.

'Perhaps you don't,' he agreed softly. 'And how can we find out if that's true?' She knew she had pushed him too far as he hauled her roughly to her feet with arms that shook, moving her over to the huge old trunk of the massive cedar tree standing majestically still in the dim light. He positioned them out of sight behind the ancient tree, its solid trunk as thick as a small hut.

'Now then, you were saying?' he asked thickly as she shrank from the fury in his gaze.

'Leave me alone,' she said weakly as he moved in front of her, blocking out the moonlight with his big body as he backed her against the rough bark, its harsh surface scratching her bare back.

'You try my patience again and again,' he muttered softly. 'I can't believe you don't know what you are doing.' She

247

stared at his shadowed face in the dim light. There was no softness or tenderness in the piercing blue gaze that locked swords with her soft grey eyes, no response to the frightened appeal in her face.

'Please, Dimitrios, stop this now,' she begged, putting out a tentative hand and touching his cheek with light fingers that shook. His face relaxed, a strange expression flickering into his eyes as he looked down at her slight figure enclosed in his arms, his body stirring against her softness.

'What are we doing to each other?' he muttered, shaking his dark head in restless longing. 'I've let you get under my skin.' His gentleness unnerved her more than his fierce desire; she could fight against his fury but this seductive tenderness was weakening her shaky resolve.

'I want you,' he said with a touch of his old arrogance. 'That can't be wrong, can it?' He pulled her into the hard lines of his body as he spoke, claiming her mouth in a long hungry kiss before she could answer, his need blatant.

Her body answered his immediately, and as he moved his burning lips frantically over her face and throat she felt herself responding to his lovemaking in a manner as old as time. Sensing her submission, he moved her away from the tree, although she was hardly aware of it until he was resting against the scented wood, only the firm pressure of his arms keeping her against him, his breathing ragged as he ran his hands down her pliant body. 'I think I could learn to live with your dislike,' he said mockingly, his eyes warm. She tried to make herself move away, sensing in that moment that he had purposely given her a means of escape, but instead she found herself wrapping her arms more tightly round his neck as he gathered her close, drinking in the intoxicating male smell and feel of his big body.

'You know how I feel?' he questioned unsteadily, and she lowered her head in reply, the fall of her hair hiding her flushed face in a shimmering veil.

'It's not enough, is it?' Her voice trembled and she felt him stiffen against her. There had to be more than stolen moments for her. If she gave herself to him it would be a lifelong commitment and he had already promised that to someone else. She wanted all of him, not just his body.

'Listen to me, Ria,' he said huskily, 'there is something I must explain. Something you have to understand.' He pushed her away from him slightly as he spoke and she felt cold all over.

Her thoughts raced madly. He was going to tell her about Kristie. Not that, she couldn't bear hearing that now. 'No!' she said wildly, taking a step backwards, her face panic-stricken, 'I don't want to hear it. Nothing you could say to me would make any difference. It's too late.'

'I see.' His voice was grim. 'Then it would appear that I have made a fool of myself.'

'No.' She moved to touch his arm but something in the proud rigid face held her hand. 'You couldn't do that.'

'No kindness, Ria.' His voice was a cold warning. 'I have never been so near to taking a woman by force in my life. Get back to the others now.' The big body was motionless.

She stared at him, appalled by the pain in his voice. 'Dimitrios, you don't understand—'

'I said go.' For an endless moment they stared at each other in locked misery, the party sounds in the distance a subtle mockery to them both.

As she still stood frozen before him he brushed violently past her with a muttered oath, walking back into the lights without a backward glance.

She followed him out of the black concealing shadows on legs that shook, joining the others in a dull daze, unable to respond with more than monosyllables to any attempts at conversation. Frank was nowhere to be seen, for which she was grateful; his friendly face would have been the last straw for nerves which were stretched to breaking point.

She was unaware that Dimitrios was never far from her side, his eyes tight and watchful on her white vacant face and his mouth a straight grim line.

Poppy joined her after a few minutes, looking unusually tired in the vivid light from the lanterns. 'Where on earth have you been?' she asked worriedly, her eyes sharp. 'You look absolutely terrible; what's happened?'

'Nothing,' Ria answered woodenly and her cousin snorted in disbelief.

'You mean to say you vanish for over an hour with our esteemed master and then return looking like death warmed up and nothing happened?'

'Please, Poppy.' It was only two words but Poppy realised her cousin was at the end of her tether.

'Nikos has ordered a taxi for us. I was going to say you didn't have to come with me now, but perhaps you'd like to?' Her voice was gentle.

'Yes, please.'

Ria really only came to herself as the taxi drew up outside the villa, the harsh barking of the dogs breaking through the daze that had brushed over her mind.

'Right.' Poppy's voice was brusque as she steered Ria away from the stairs as they walked in, and through to the silent shadowed lounge where a small lamp had been left burning in the blackness. 'We're not moving from here until you tell me what's going on, and don't you dare say "nothing" again.'

One of the smaller dogs crept stealthily on to Ria's lap as she lay back in her chair with a soft sigh, and the comforting warmth of the small furry body warmed her cold limbs as she stared at her cousin in the dim light.

'You needn't look at me like that.' Poppy's voice was determined. 'I mean

252

it, I want to know what's going on. What an evening!' she expostulated. 'First of all Dimitrios practically assaults one of the men he threw the party for in the first place. Nikos just couldn't believe his eyes. He's quite convinced his uncle has flipped his lid.'

'It was only Frank.' Ria's voice was low and Poppy looked at her impatiently.

'What on earth did the poor man do to deserve all that?'

'Nothing, really,' Ria replied, her voice weary.

'If you say that word once more I'll scream,' Poppy said tightly. 'I can't believe Dimitrios behaved like that, it was so embarrassing. And then he whipped you away, glaring at everyone as though we'd committed a cardinal sin by being there in the first place and then the pair of you disappear from the face of the earth for an hour, and when you came back—well!' Words seemed to fail her and she looked at Ria indignantly.

'You looked like death and he looked as though someone had punched him in the stomach. What on earth is going on, Ria? And don't you *dare* say nothing.'

'It's all such a mess,' Ria whispered

slowly with a little sob in her voice. 'Such an awful mess.'

'Well, I know I'm not much cop as family but I'm all you've got and I'm on your side right or wrong.' Poppy's pixie face was earnestly sincere and she clasped hold of Ria's hands in a rare show of affection. 'Come on, tell me.'

'Promise me you won't tell a soul?' urged Ria brokenly, and as her cousin nodded her agreement she looked away into the quiet darkness. 'Dimitrios is going to marry Kristie.' The stark empty words hung in the air for a frozen moment before Poppy let out her breath in a low loud hiss.

'I don't believe it,' she said firmly.

'It's true, Poppy.'

'Who told you? Not her?' As Ria nodded her cousin jumped up in agitation, beginning to pace up and down in front of her in restless impatience. 'Honestly, Ria, you are so gullible it's not true,' she said caustically. 'She's been after him for years and since you arrived on the scene it's clear she's got desperate. Nikos says his uncle has never acted like this in all his life before; if he can see the signs you can bet Kristie can.'

'You don't understand,' Ria said wearily, 'it's not the way you think. Dimitrios knew a girl once, Caroline, she broke his heart when he was very young and he's never forgiven her as far as I can see. Maybe he still loves her, I don't know. Anyway, she looked exactly like me. Now do you see? He only wants me because I resemble her, not because there is any affection there.'

'Codswallop!' said Poppy sharply. 'Dimitrios isn't some young boy to be swayed by your looks and if you believe that you're more stupid than I thought. I'm sorry, Ria,' she continued as she saw her stricken face, 'but I just don't believe he intends to marry Kristie. Have you asked him?'

Ria shook her head miserably. 'How can I do that when Kristie told me in confidence? Not even Christina knows yet. They're going to wait till after your wedding to announce it, and I've seen the ring anyway. It would have cost thousands.'

A small glimmer of doubt appeared in Poppy's eyes for an instant but then she shook her head adamantly. 'There's got to be a reasonable explanation for that; I just don't believe Dimitrios would let himself be trapped by that little conniving... Perhaps she borrowed the ring from someone?'

'It's you who's being stupid now,' said Ria softly. 'No one lends something like that; we're talking about a small fortune. Face it, Poppy, she suits him far better than I would.'

Poppy looked at her with growing anxiety. 'You've got to fight, Ria. You know you love him; don't let it all slip away.'

'I haven't got your tenacity,' Ria replied, 'besides which there is nothing to fight for. He's made his choice and maybe it's best for both of us.'

Poppy gave one of her snorts of disgust. 'Tell me another! I've never seen you so miserable and if he's supposed to have asked Kristie to marry him it hasn't exactly made him ecstatic, has it? You both look ill.'

'Just leave it, Poppy,' Ria protested quietly. 'I shall be gone in a few days and then you can all get on with your lives and I can pick up the pieces of mine.'

'And that's supposed to make me feel good?' Poppy's voice was pleading. 'Let me ask him, Ria, in a roundabout sort of way? I can—'

'I promise you that if you say a word to

anyone about this I shall forget I ever knew you.' Ria's voice was as cold as ice and for once Poppy didn't argue, subsiding in hurt silence as Ria rose slowly and left the room, walking like an old woman, every vestige of her being proclaiming defeat.

The next morning Kristie arrived back with an armful of wedding-presents which Poppy accepted with surly bad grace. The redhead's sharp green eyes narrowed at the other girl's lack of enthusiasm and she flicked her carefully coiffured head spitefully. 'Wedding nerves?' she drawled, her venomous gaze tight on Poppy's angry red face.

'No!' Poppy snapped tightly, her eyes shooting sparks, and Kristie laughed softly as she turned and lifted another package from the flood of suitcases the perspiring taxi driver had hauled in a few minutes before.

'A little something for Christina,' she said indifferently to no one in particular. 'I suppose she's in her room?'

'Yes, and the men are at work,' said Poppy, her low voice loaded with sarcasm, flushing slightly as she caught Ria's warning gaze from across the room.

'I can see you are still as busy as

a little bee,' Kristie said mockingly to Ria as she caught her steady grey gaze, and as Ria held her glance making no reply she flushed bright pink, turning away with a slight flounce in her step. 'Friendly this morning, aren't we?' she drawled sardonically over her shoulder as she walked towards the staircase with slow elegance. 'So nice to see you back, Kristie; did you have a good journey, Kristie?'

'Drop dead, Kristie,' Poppy muttered under her breath as the redhead sauntered up the staircase, trailing a languid hand over the smooth polished wood of the curved banister, and wandering along the wide sunlit landing to Christina's room.

As the day progressed Ria found her nerves winding tighter and tighter. The cool green gaze seemed to burn into her forehead until she could have screamed, raising her eyes suddenly from the lists she was checking to find Kristie's slanted eyes watching her every move, the beautiful face coldly speculative. 'You hate me, don't you?' Kristie could have been asking for a cup of coffee, so bland was her voice.

'Why should I hate you?' Ria looked away and down at the typewritten sheets in her hands, her stomach lurching at the abrupt confrontation.

'You know why,' said Kristie haughtily, her voice like the first flurry of icy hailstones before a storm. 'Why don't you just give up and go back home while you've still got some pride left? I have to say I didn't expect to find you still here when I got back.'

'Sorry to disappoint you,' said Ria, her calm, expressionless voice clearly irritating the other woman still further.

'Don't think you fool me for a moment with that innocent little girl routine,' Kristie spat, moving closer to where Ria sat and looking down at her, green eyes malevolent. 'You might have fooled Dimitrios but I've got you taped. You're nothing but a common little gold-digger but, believe me, there's no point in you hanging on here. You'll be out on your ear once this wedding is over so you might just as well pack your bags and clear out now.'

'I'll go when I'm ready,' said Ria clearly, raising her eyes and meeting Kristie's spiteful gaze head on. Their glances locked and held for a few seconds, and it was Kristie who dropped her eyes first, her face ugly with hate.

'I've seen plenty like you come and go,'

she hissed over her shoulder as she turned away, her eyes shooting green sparks. 'You might last for a month or two but he soon loses interest. I'm the one he comes back to and don't you forget it.'

'I've no intention of "lasting" for any amount of time,' Ria said coolly, her voice belying her churning stomach. She stood up and walked towards the staircase, her voice low but perfectly controlled as she added, 'I pity Dimitrios, getting a wife like you, I pity him with all my heart.'

'Save it!' Kristie's voice was biting and there was a flash of triumph lighting her face as she watched Ria leave the room, her smooth white hands curled into red-tipped talons by her side. 'Save your pity for yourself; you'll need it for all those long cold nights when you imagine him loving me.'

Ria managed to reach her room before her legs gave way and she sank trembling on to the bed. The sheer viciousness of the attack had left her breathless; she had never encountered such pure undiluted hate before. Perhaps it would be best if she left now. One thing was certain, Kristie was determined to make things as unpleasant as possible.

Her mind was made up by the time she went down for dinner later that evening. Some perverse pride had made her take special care with her appearance and she had brushed her thick hair until it shone like molten silver, looping it up into a loose knot on the top of her head with silky tendrils falling in soft appeal round her smooth neck, her eyes wide and faintly shadowed.

They were all sitting in the lounge as she descended the stairs and she felt a familiar dart of pain as she noticed Kristie's red head close in conversation with Dimitrios's, her hand resting possessively on his arm. She hadn't seen him since the barbecue the night before and her stomach tightened as he raised his head lazily, the dark blue eyes sweeping over her body and up to her face in mocking appraisal.

'Drink?' The deep voice was soft and she trembled fleetingly.

'Thank you, a dry sherry, please.' She found herself unable to look at Kristie but was acutely aware of the redhead's slim pliant body unfolding against Dimitrios as he stood up to get her drink. The insidious way Kristie wrapped herself round her brother was not lost on Christina either. The older woman's eyes were coldly disapproving as she watched Dimitrios pour Ria's drink, mellowing only slightly as after handing her the drink he remained standing by her chair, talking generally with the others until Rosa announced dinner was ready.

Rosa's expert culinary talents were wasted on Ria that night. Everything tasted like sawdust in her mouth and every cell in her body was painfully aware that this would probably be the last time she would eat at this table. It was as they began dessert that she dropped her bombshell. Poppy had unwittingly given her the lead as she turned to Ria in a lull in the conversation, putting her hand on her cousin's arm.

'Can you come with me to the cottage tomorrow?' she asked clearly. 'I want to fix up the curtains and have a last clean round and I thought it would be good for us to get away for a day.' She flashed a hard glance at Kristie as she spoke and the other woman's eyes sparkled in contemptuous amusement.

'I'm sorry, Poppy.' There was a tremor in Ria's voice but her face was calm and controlled as she answered. 'I'm going back home tomorrow. I've been away long enough and Julian can't keep my job open indefinitely.'

If she had suddenly taken all her clothes off and danced naked on the table the result couldn't have been more dramatic than the reaction her softly spoken words caused.

She knew Poppy was staring at her in horror and Christina's face was deeply concerned, but her eyes were glued on Dimitrios as he sprang up from the table so suddenly that his chair went spinning out behind him in a whirling arc. 'What do you mean?' His eyes were tight on her white face. 'You promised to stay until the wedding; I didn't think you would break your word.'

'I promised to stay until all the arrangements were completed, and they are,' Ria corrected quietly, her eyes caught and held by the dark anger in his. 'I want to go home.'

There was such a poignant plea in her last words that it reached everyone, even the red-haired American sitting so complacently by Dimitrios's side. Kristie's eyes shifted uncomfortably for a moment as she looked up at his dark face as he leant on the table, both hands flat on the hard surface, his expression one of livid fury.

'You aren't leaving,' he rapped out, seemingly unaware of anyone else present. 'I won't let you.'

'I am.' She answered in the same vein, her eyes locked into his and her face pale and frightened as he walked round the table to where she sat.

'Get up.' His voice was menacingly quiet and brought a quick exclamation from Christina as she too rose and came to Ria's side.

'Leave the child alone, Dimitrios. If she wants to go home of course she must be allowed to do so.' His sister's voice seemed to bring some sort of normality back to his face, and he turned to Christina, his gaze withering.

'I only want to talk to her in private.'

'I don't want to talk to you.' As she spoke the words up into his face she saw a pain that was reflected in her own heart rip through his austere features and turn his eyes into chips of granite as he straightened slowly.

He stared at her for a long moment, his eyes seeking to reach into her mind. 'And Christina?' he asked at last, his face now supremely arrogant and bitterly proud. 'You think she can cope without your help on the wedding day?'

'I wouldn't be leaving if I was unsure,' she said brokenly.

'So be it.' He spoke as if pronouncing a death sentence. 'Go back to England, Ria, go back there and rot.'

'Dimitrios!' At Christina's startled protest he swung round on his sister, his face as black as thunder.

'She is not welcome in my home again. Remember that if you value your well-being.' As Christina stared aghast at him he gave a twisted smile that turned his face into a distorted caricature, and, clicking his fingers sharply at the dogs sleeping on the veranda, he left the room unhurriedly through the large windows into the dark garden.

Kristie went to follow him but at a sharp command from Christina she sank back down in her seat, green eyes flashing sulkily. 'I can't see what all the fuss is about,' she muttered softly. 'She's only leaving a few days early and, as she said, she only stayed on to take care of the wedding arrangements.'

'Shut your mouth.' Poppy had left her seat now and was virtually crouching over

Kristie like an enraged goblin, her small face bright red with anger. 'You've done enough damage.'

'Poppy.' Ria's voice was pleading and Kristie's narrowed eyes flashed from one cousin to another.

'How sweet,' she drawled mockingly. 'Blood thicker than water and all that rubbish?'

'You think you're very clever, don't you?' spat Poppy as she irritably shook off Nikos's restraining hand from her arm. 'Well, maybe you're a sight too clever, you old cat.'

'Poppy!' This time Nikos's voice was joined to Ria's and as Christina subsided into a vacant seat, her face suddenly grey and beads of perspiration standing out on her forehead, all attention was focused on the older woman. As Ria anxiously rubbed Christina's hands, trying to put some warmth into the cold flesh, Nikos poured a glass of brandy and put it to his mother's white lips, and Poppy hovered between the two, her young face frightened.

After a few minutes some colour seeped back into Christina's pale face and she smiled shakily. 'I think we could all do with an early night,' she said slowly, her eyes warm on Ria's desolate face. 'Could I ask one last favour, my dear?'

As Ria nodded uncertainly the older woman covered her hand with her own. 'I hate to ask, but could you go with Poppy tomorrow and finish getting the house ready? It would be a weight off my mind to know everything is finished and I don't want Poppy straining to hang up curtains at this stage in her pregnancy. I promise you I will personally arrange a seat on the first available flight after tomorrow. Please, Ria?'

Ria nodded again. She was hurting badly and knew the healing process would never begin until she was away from this place and its dark owner, but she owed Christina one more day.

'Just tomorrow,' she agreed, her voice painfully acquiescent, wincing slightly as Kristie flounced out of the room with an exaggerated sigh.

Christina smiled gently, her eyes hovering on Poppy for a moment before they returned to the pale slim girl in front of her. 'Just tomorrow,' she repeated. 'You have my word. Everything will be sorted out by then.'

CHAPTER TEN

The small house was as beautiful as Ria remembered, slumbering peacefully in the morning's heat when they arrived the next day. Nikos left after opening all the newly painted windows wide to banish the sickly odour of paint and warning them to take it easy.

Ria set to work immediately, forcing her mind on the task in hand with relentless determination. Dimitrios had already left for the plant when the rest of the house woke that morning; Rosa had informed them at breakfast that he hadn't slept in his bed at all. Nikos had bolted his breakfast, chivvying Poppy and Ria along unmercifully, clearly not looking forward to the day ahead in his uncle's company and then grumbling furiously when his mother had kept Poppy in her room for ten minutes checking catering arrangements.

'I thought that was all done,' he had complained to Poppy when she joined him and Ria in the car, bright-eyed and flushed. 'Dimitrios is going to kill me for being late.'

'I doubt it.' Poppy's voice was almost light-hearted. 'Christina has got to phone him later about certain arrangements and she'll explain we kept you waiting.'

After hanging the pretty flowered curtains, Ria helped Poppy to arrange the furniture downstairs. Dimitrios had been extremely generous, giving them a free hand with the furnishings, and Poppy had had a wonderful time spending lavishly with her usual flamboyance. By mid-afternoon the small house had blossomed into a home, gleaming and welcoming.

'Has Uncle John confirmed whether he is coming?' asked Ria as they were finishing cleaning the small leaded windows that so added to the cottage's character.

'No. I don't want him to, anyway,' Poppy answered dismissively, her face hard.

'Oh, come on, Poppy,' Ria remonstrated gently, but her cousin wouldn't be persuaded.

'I haven't got your gift of turning the other cheek,' she said tightly. 'He hasn't bothered about me all my life so I don't expect him to start now.' Ria shrugged regretfully; there were some things better left untouched.

They collapsed exhausted in two easy-chairs in the small hot garden in the late afternoon. The air was sluggish, the leaden sky a pale brilliant grey that spoke of an impending storm. The electricity in the air always affected Ria strangely, causing her head to ache and her nerve-endings to jangle irritably, and today was worse than ever with her thoughts churning constantly towards the tall dark figure who haunted her mind.

'Oh, no! We're out of drink,' Poppy remembered after a few minutes. 'Do you think you can last until Nikos picks us up later?'

'I'll walk down into the town if you like and see if anywhere is open,' Ria offered. 'The siesta should be finishing now, and there must be somewhere I can buy a bottle of lemonade.' As she closed the small front door behind her a few minutes later she heard the first ominous warning of low storm growls rumbling in the dense sky, and the heavy humid air seemed to press down on to her head, causing a trickle of panic to race down her spine.

'Don't be a baby,' she told herself

loudly, fighting down the weakness that thunder always produced in her, trying to ignore the swiftly darkening sky. There had been a particularly violent storm the day her family had been killed, and in spite of cold reason telling her it was just a quirk of nature the ferocity of a storm always made her into a frightened seven-year-old again, rolling back the intervening years as though they were the blink of an eye.

She had to venture quite a way into the sleepy town before she found a shop that was open, and after swiftly completing her purchases, she stepped out into the thick air as the first enormous raindrops began to fall.

She was halfway back to the cottage when the world erupted around her. Vivid white flashes of lightning rent the sky apart with majestic savagery and the crash of thunder was like a bomb overhead, lifting her off her feet with its volume. A solid sheet of rain turned the ordinary street into an alien world, stinging her face and blinding her eyes, her ears still ringing with the vibration of noise as she began to stumble along, unable to see a hand in front of her.

She wouldn't have believed a storm could

be so violent, but as a vivid thunderbolt seemed to pass directly through her she dropped the lemonade unconsciously, flinging her hands over her ears and starting to run blindly down the middle of the road which had turned into a river of water.

As she neared the crossroads leading into Poppy's street she thought she caught a glimpse of a tall dark figure shouting to her in the distance but then another savage crash of thunder obliterated all sense of reason, and she rushed madly across the junction. For one frozen moment in time she saw the huge truck almost upon her, its driver's mouth agape, and then she was flung upwards like a small rag doll. As the ground rushed towards her a million little arrows began striking her body again and again and then it all faded into a noisy red haze, the rain beating down on to her upturned face.

Disembodied voices were calling her name urgently as the pain surfaced, ripping through her so fiercely that she lost the power to breathe. She was vaguely aware of a strong pair of arms cradling her head and a hoarse frantic voice calling her name, but thankfully the pain and noise began to recede as she let herself fall into the dark void of unconsciousness opening out beneath her.

She came round once in the ambulance as it sped along, sirens screaming, and could hear the sound of sobbing in the background as someone stroked her head, gently whispering her name. It hurt too much to try to remain in that land and she slipped back gratefully into the dark mantle that was covering her again, its blackness consuming.

The next time she surfaced she knew something was different. The fire that had been eating her up and torturing her dreams had gone out and a cool breeze was playing on her face. She wanted to open her eyes but her lids were too heavy; they were weighing her down and pushing her back into the softness, the gentle comforting softness that was cushioning her aching limbs.

She heard a rustling at her side and something cold was placed on her hot forehead. 'Ria?' The deep masculine voice was a tortured groan. 'Darling, fight it, don't let go. I love you, my angel. Open your eyes, Ria.' She tried to obey but the pain in her head was overwhelming and she searched for that deep blackness again. She was so tired, so deathly tired.

When she woke again the room was in semi-darkness, a small night-light burning to one side of the bed. She felt drowsy but the paralysing exhaustion was gone and her body belonged to her again. She glanced round carefully; her head was pounding but she dimly recalled it aching far worse.

The small clinically clean room smelt strongly of antiseptic and as she tried to move she realised with horror that her legs were encased in a giant metal contraption at the end of the narrow bed, and she whimpered, panic-stricken.

'It's all right, don't move, my love, everything's all right.' Dimitrios had been asleep in an easy chair just behind her line of vision and now he almost fell to kneel at her side, his dark face thick with black stubble and his blue eyes red rimmed.

'Where am I?' she whispered dazedly, the pain in her head beginning to throb again.

'You're in hospital, my sweet,' he replied softly, his voice shaking, and she looked hard at him, trying to see the expression on his face.

'Oh, yes, the storm,' she murmured as

she sank back into sleep. When she next opened her eyes it was growing light outside and Dimitrios was still kneeling in the same position at her side, his head resting on the white coverlet, fast asleep. For the first time since she had known him his clothes were rumpled and creased, with what looked like dried blood caking the front of his shirt.

She moved slightly and he was awake in an instant, his blue eyes sharply alert. 'Ria?'

'I'm sorry,' she whispered, 'I seem to have caused a lot of trouble.'

'It's your second name,' he smiled with a shaky attempt at humour. 'How do you feel?'

'As if I've been run over by a lorry,' she smiled back, and as he caught her eyes he gave a chuckle that turned into what sounded suspiciously like a sob.

'I thought I'd lost you.' He was covering her face with gentle, feather-light kisses, murmuring her name over and over again as he gathered her carefully into his arms. 'Oh, my darling.'

'Dimitrios?' She tried to pull away to see his face but caught her breath as a shaft of pain shot through her chest, and he immediately rang the small bell at the side of the bed.

'Don't move,' he said urgently, his eyes incredibly tender as a middle aged white-coated doctor opened the door and moved swiftly over to where Ria lay.

'Hi, young lady.' The doctor's voice was very English and his bearded face was smiling as he looked down at her, preparing a syringe as he spoke. 'I'm just going to put you back to sleep again for a short time and when you wake up you'll feel like a million dollars.'

As the injection pierced her arm Ria shut her eyes tiredly, a hundred questions churning in her head. 'She's out of danger now, Mr Koutsoupis,' the voice continued quietly, 'and it's time you obeyed orders and took some rest. You didn't have me flown out from England to ignore me, now, did you? I don't want two patients to deal with.'

She heard Dimitrios say something very rude as the waves of slumber took over and then all was quiet.

Bright golden sunlight was flooding the small room when she awoke and she was alone. She lay quietly before ringing the bell at her side, trying to collect her thoughts, confused between what was reality and her wild dreams. 'He couldn't have,' she whispered disbelievingly into the shaft of golden light falling across her face. 'He couldn't have said he loved me.'

A small dark nurse answered the bell immediately, her round face bright and friendly, only too ready to fill in the missing gaps in Ria's memory. 'Mr Koutsoupis raised the whole hospital when they brought you in,' she said cheerfully in excellent English. 'He was shouting at everyone, insisting nothing was good enough, and refused to leave your side even when they X-rayed you. Your cousin couldn't do a thing with him, although she was pretty hysterical herself.' Ria smiled to herself; that sounded like Dimitrios.

'He determined there was no one qualified enough to treat you properly, and offended the whole hierarchy here by calling out Dr Nicholls from England to personally supervise your recovery. He's the top man in head injuries.'

Ria touched her head gingerly.

'It's all right,' the nurse said reassuringly, seeing the gesture, 'you're over the concussion now but it was a bit touch and go for a time. They weren't too sure what was

277

happening in there.' She smiled warmly at Ria. 'The only thing you've got to contend with now is a cracked rib and two broken legs. You were very lucky; it could have been a lot worse.'

'It could?' said Ria wryly. She felt as though her whole body was one giant ache.

'I'll go and see about a meal for you,' the nurse offered, as she finished brushing Ria's hair. 'You've missed lunch but I can rustle up some soup and rolls.'

'That's very kind, but don't go to a lot of trouble,' Ria said quickly. 'I'm not really hungry.'

'Oh, we've got to keep you happy,' the nurse replied, the slight bite in her words softened by a warm smile. 'Mr Koutsoupis has frightened us all to death.' Ria grinned in reply, both girls' expressions freezing as a deep cold voice spoke from the open doorway.

'Thank you, Nurse. I won't keep you.' The nurse darted a quick grimace at Ria before turning and leaving the room at a trot, shutting the door firmly behind her.

Dimitrios stood just by the door, restored to his usual immaculate self, but white lines of strain and exhaustion stood out clearly on his dark face and his eyes were shadowed.

'Hello.' Ria lowered her eyes as she spoke, feeling suddenly desperately shy.

'Forgive me?' His voice was thick and strange and he remained quite still, a tall black statue in the white sunlit room. 'I've no right to ask but I'll get down on my knees if it will help you to understand.'

She stared at his tormented face with something akin to horror in her soft grey eyes. 'I don't want you on your knees,' she said gently, and he groaned in reply.

'I brought you to yours, though, didn't I? I can't believe how blind and stupid I've been.' He took a step towards her and then visibly restrained himself, bunching his hands deep in his pockets. 'I must talk to you, make you see why I behaved as I did, and if I touch you I shan't be able to.'

'I understand,' said Ria softly. 'Christina told me about Caroline and—'

'You don't understand!' He bit the words out through clenched teeth, his face grim. 'When I first saw you, there in the flat that day, I admit you reminded me of Caroline and with all that Nikos had told me it seemed as though fate had

279

dropped another promiscuous silver-haired siren into my life to be a source of pain and irritation and worse.' He breathed deeply, his face white.

'But you didn't add up. I couldn't work out how this cool, gentle girl that I clearly frightened half to death could be the conniving, experienced woman of the world that Nikos had described. I knew Nikos had slept with his girlfriend and yet when I held you in my arms you responded so innocently, you were so obviously out of your depth and trying to cope with emotions new to you, that I didn't know what to believe.' He turned away, walking over to the window and standing with his back towards her, his black hair shining blue in the sunlight.

'The day on the beach I'd finally decided I didn't care any more. I had to have you whatever you were like, I made the decision to take a chance and trust my heart, but I had to see you with Nikos first to make sure it was really over. When I found out you'd been fooling me for days, that all my torment had been unnecessary...' He shook his head in confusion. 'I think I went mad for a while.'

'I'm sorry—' Ria began hesitantly, tears running down her face, but he stopped her abruptly, still keeping his back to her.

'No, let me finish. It's got to be said.' His voice was raw with emotion. 'It was all my fault, you see. I knew even before I found out you weren't Poppy that you were sweet and kind, that I could love you for the rest of my life. After that first shock you didn't even remind me of Caroline any more. Apart from the physical resemblance you were such opposites—she never had your softness or purity—but something deep inside couldn't let go. I had to test you again and again even though I knew I was hurting you, destroying any hope I had with you.'

He turned towards her now, his eyes grief-stricken. 'I asked you to stay and help with the wedding because I couldn't bear to let you go. I wanted you near me and yet I couldn't believe you could love me, trust me, not after the way I'd treated you. You gave yourself to me so sweetly time and time again and I just threw it back in your face...'

She held out her arms towards him, unable to stand the pain in his face any longer. 'No more,' she whispered, her hair wet with the tears dripping down her face. 'Please, Dimitrios, no more.'

'How can you want me?' He still didn't move. 'Christina told me what Kristie had said; Poppy confided in her the morning of the accident. I was away from the plant but when I got back in the afternoon she called me and explained and I came straight over to the cottage. I was too late.' His face twisted. 'When I saw your body hit the ground...'

'I thought I saw you,' said Ria slowly, her arms still outstretched towards him.

'It was all lies, Ria, about Kristie. She is—was—a friend, nothing more.' His voice was grim. 'She confessed to Christina that she had bought the ring herself; money is no object to her when she has a scheme in hand. The divorce settlement was very generous.'

He moved suddenly to her side and, with a smothered exclamation, gathered her gently into his arms, kissing her hungrily until she gasped for breath against his hard mouth. 'I'm sorry, I'm too rough,' he said thickly, 'but you've no idea how I've longed to do that over the last few days. Can you forgive me? Learn to love me, maybe?'

'I don't need to learn,' Ria sobbed against his broad chest. 'I've loved you almost from the first moment I saw you but I didn't think you could ever love me.' Her eyes were anguished as she remembered his mercurial changes of mood in the past.

He took her face in his hands, bringing her eyes into line with his, which were lit with such tenderness and hope that she hardly dared breathe. 'I will never love anyone the way I love you,' he said slowly, his breathing ragged. 'You are my sun, moon and stars. I want you to be my wife, to bear my children and for us to grow old together. If you don't accept me there will never be anyone in my life again and I will have nothing to live for.' His intensity thrilled her even as it frightened her and she pulled him close against her body. Never in her wildest dreams had she imagined hearing such words from the cold, arrogant man she had come to love.

With a low animal groan he captured her lips again, moving his hands possessively over her body as his mouth devoured hers until he pulled away suddenly, his arms trembling.

'You haven't answered me,' he said

shakily, his eyes burning. 'Will you be my wife?'

'For always,' she whispered lovingly, ''till death us do part.'

He filled his hands with the silky folds of her silver hair. 'So beautiful and all mine,' he said triumphantly, his eyes gleaming with desire. 'I hope you heal quickly, my love; I'm not a patient man.'

Ria looked at him, her heart in her eyes. 'Have you forgiven me for all the mistakes I made at the beginning?' she asked softly, her face glowing with love.

'There's nothing to forgive.' His voice was tender. 'What you did, you did out of love and concern for Poppy; I knew that all along and love you all the more for it. Let's just say a case of mistaken identity was the culprit, and it's something I shall thank God for all the rest of my life.'

And he did.

This Large Print Book for the Partially sighted, who cannot read normal print, is published under the auspices of

THE ULVERSCROFT FOUNDATION

THE ULVERSCROFT FOUNDATION

. . . we hope that you have enjoyed this Large Print Book. Please think for a moment about those people who have worse eyesight problems than you . . . and are unable to even read or enjoy Large Print, without great difficulty.

You can help them by sending a donation, large or small to:

**The Ulverscroft Foundation,
1, The Green, Bradgate Road,
Anstey, Leicestershire, LE7 7FU,
England.**
or request a copy of our brochure for more details.

The Foundation will use all your help to assist those people who are handicapped by various sight problems and need special attention.

Thank you very much for your help.